MIDST OF MY CONFUSION

MIDST OF MY CONFUSION

A STORY OF LIFE, DEATH & REVOLUTION

DAVID ROCHA

Parakletos Publishing

Tracy

Dedication

Dedicated to my parents
Roberto y Erminia Rocha
Everything I do is for my Familia

Contents

Introduction

First, allow me to thank you for reading this book that I wrote many years ago. So much has happened since I wrote the book while on House Arrest back in 1999 for a drug case I was arrested and convicted for. I was again arrested in 2000 by the F.B.I. under RICO charges, and then while on bail for that case I was again arrested for drug trafficking on FEB 25th, 2004. I was given an 8-year prison sentence in Federal Prison and that is where my life was dramatically changed.

I was raised in a Christian home and had no desire to be a Christian myself. So I lived my life as I wanted and became a very popular recording artist in the Chicano Rap genre. I was living the so-called 'life' that many desire to have yet I found myself very empty. So after many arrests, I found myself in the Sacramento County Jail in solitary confinement and looking into the scratched mirror I didn't like what I saw. I had lost all morals and who I was. So like my father before me, I asked the Lord Jesus Christ into my life, I repented of my sins and the most amazing thing happened. The weight of violence, hate, anger, greed, manipulation lifted off my body instantly. There is no way to describe the feeling but I knew God was real. I went head first into reading a Bible given to me by a sheriff and the renewing of my mind began. I spent the next two years in a cell and one of those years in solitary confinement. I became a sponge for the Word of God and after fifteen months I felt the call to preach His Word to all people that I would come across while in prison and in the free world. After two years of living in a cell, I was transported to Terminal Island Federal Correctional Facility in Long Beach CA. I began to preach in the yard there and lead a group of other Christian men. During the last two years of my sentence, I was eligible to be transported to a Federal prison camp, which I did in Atwater in northern California. During my stay there I enrolled at Christian Leadership University, and through correspondence, I earned my Associates degree in Biblical Studies and was licensed and ordained by C.R.F.I. before I was released. I was finally free from Federal Prison (BOP) on Jan 20th, 2010 and am now a Pastor in Modesto CA. The church name is House of Rest which is under the covering of Grace International and our website is www.houseofrestchurch.com.

I also chose to publish this book as a digital eBook, because of the many fans from my past that requested it, also as a bridge from my past to where I am now. A bridge that I hope was built for many to cross over. For you, the reader, to understand that there is a God, and He loves you very much. The Bible says that He is like a shepherd looking for His lost sheep, calling out your name until He finds you. And when He does, He rejoices and puts you over his shoulder and carries you home. It doesn't cost anything and He takes you the way you are. All you have to do is ask Him. Please feel free to go to our website and email me personally if you have any questions. Thank you. www.houseofrestchurch.com

Prologue

Emiliano Zapata
August 8, 1879- April 10, 1919
Emiliano Zapata was a Mexican revolutionary, leader of the division of the South of Mexico during the Mexican Revolution of 1910. Emiliano Zapata campaigned for the restoration of village lands confiscated by hacendados. His

slogan was "Tierra y Libertad." As a result of an ambush, Zapata was betrayed and murdered. Zapata will continue to live as long as people believe that they have a right to their land and a right to govern themselves according to their deeply held beliefs and cultural values.

"I'd rather die on my feet than to live on my knees"
Emiliano Zapata

Pancho Villa
June 5, 1878 – July 23, 1923
Pancho Villa became a fugitive when he killed his landlord for sexually attacking his sister. He then fled to the mountains. He later joined the uprising of 1910 and became the most ruthless general of the Mexican Revolution. He was a warrior who fought for the sake of fighting. He took revenge against the rich and powerful in the name of those deprived of their rights. Pancho Villa's life was littered with corpses. As General of the Northern division of Mexico, he was feared. Villa's charisma drew to himself thousands of adventurers, landless people, and pistoleros. He was

ambushed and killed in a shoot-out. He died with his pistol in hand.

Subcomandante Marcos
Spokesman for EZLN
Zapatistas

On new year's eve, in 1994, indigenous rebels in masks rose up in arms in the state of Chiapas, Mexico, occupying the city San Cristobal, the political, economic and religious center of the indigenous highlands. They chose the name Zapatistas after the revolutionary hero Emiliano Zapata. Tired of the unfair treatment by the government, men, and women trained in the jungles of Chiapas and risked their lives for equality. Fighting between the EZLN and the Mexican army still continues to this present day. Men and women are kidnapped, murdered and jailed. Weapons and helicopters given to the Mexican government by the United States for the fight against Drugs are used to murder and destroy villages. The uprising of Chiapas is history in the

making. To read more about this subject go to www.ezln.org
"In Chiapas, the masked ones unmask the centers of power"
The Chiapas Rebellion by Philip L. Russell

Rodolfo 'Corky' Gonzales
1928 -2005.
His life's mission was to improve the lives of Chicanos
and to instill a sense of pride in Chicano heritage. As a
political activist, he founded the Crusade for Justice, an
organization that worked for social justice. The school he
founded, Escuela Tlatelolco continues today as a Denver
Public School. Corky's epic poem, "I Am Joaquin", is taught
in many university literature courses.

Preface

Thank you for choosing to read this book. I would first like to say that this is not an autobiography. I felt that this story had to be told. You might not agree with the characters you read about, but I hope it will give you a better understanding of this Chicano gang subculture embedded into our barrios. These events happen every day throughout Aztlan.
I have had the dream of writing this book for the past five years, and now finally it is done. This book is written for all of my Raza that has no voice. It's not just my story. This story belongs to all of the homeboys and homegirls that have lived this crazy life. And to those that are locked down behind prison walls, keep your head up. Those walls are only man-made, and man-made things never last forever. I would like to say R.I.P. to the many street soldiers that have died, who never had a chance in this sick twisted world.
I finished this book after being sentenced to a year for a drug charge. Something has to change out there in order for Chicanos to make it. There is something terribly wrong if we are the "minority" in the free world but the majority in the prisons. This book was a way to express myself to my fullest potential; I can only say so much in my music.

I would like to thank my editor Kika Ruda for helping me in every step of making this book happen. You helped bring out the best of me and I am forever grateful. I would also like to say thank you to everyone that's been there for me before the fame, during the fame, and after the fame. Gracias.
David Rocha

I

————————

I hear gunshots echoing in my head as if they were shot in the distance, like a dream where the faster you try to run, the slower you are. The cold air of the night is piercing my face as I run to no certain destination. I realize the gunshots are coming from the pistol in my hand. I watch as the flames of each bullet scream in slow motion looking for their victim. It feels like a nightmare I can't wake up from. I'm bleeding from a bullet shot to the stomach. I feel the burning of the bullet inside. I hear screams from frightened women, and yells from men dying. It's a yell I never want to hear again. I can sense the evil and death in the dark moonless night. Bullets whiz by so close I can feel them as they pass me by. It's nothing like the movies. When these bullets hit, there is no turning back. I find my ranfla, get in and hit the gas, almost forgetting to turn the headlights on. I can't believe I'm shot. I don't want to believe it. Deep down inside I know I had it coming.

I reach into the backseat to make sure my camcorder I

bought in Mexico is still there. I don't have much time, but there is so much I want to say. I drive toward the country, looking for a place to park. I know that if I go to the hospital, I'll go to la pinta for life. And that is no way for my story to end. I finally pull into an old abandoned barn. There's nobody in sight as I slowly step out, holding my wound with one hand. Blood is on my shirt, my hands and steering wheel. I reach into the back seat and pull out my bag with blank videotapes and camcorder. I can hardly stand the paralyzing pain in my abdomen with each step I take. As I walk towards the back of the barn I notice a small room. I quickly glance around and see a small kerosene lamp and a sink. I check and there is enough fuel to illuminate the small room. I light the wick with my lighter. I let the sink run for a few minutes until the water runs clear.

I never knew how thirsty a vato could get after getting blasted. Drinking the water gives me the strength to hold on a little longer. I rip my shirt to clean my bullet wound as best as I can. It's not as bad as I had thought, but I'm losing a lot of blood. I search the room and find a first aid kit with just enough bandages and gauze to hold back the bleeding. I sit on the old dusty couch and think of everything I've done in my life to build up to this point. I grab a new videotape and put it into the camcorder. I reach into the bag and find a fully charged battery. I want no interruptions while I tell my story. I take a long breath as I sit back and try to relax on the couch. I prop the machine on a small table facing me and push the record button.

This vida is so crazy. I guess I could try to justify all my actions to you. But instead, I'll let you be the judge of it all. Sometimes there is no right or wrong en esta vida. It all depends on the situation. Let me start from the beginning of my story, even though it's a beginning much like every Chicano I've known. Please be patient with me... I'm not a storyteller. I'm just a Crazy Vato doing what I can to survive. Let me introduce myself. I was born with the name Joaquín, but the homeboys call me Loco.

"Viva Zapata! Viva Pancho Villa!" my father would yell to me when I was a child. I would laugh and shoot into the air with my old western cap gun. I never grew up playing cowboys and Indians. For me, it was playing revolutionaries against soldiers. I loved to hear my father tell me stories about Pancho Villa.

"Pancho Villa was a big man mijo! He would take on anybody that got in his way." Then he would pick me up and hug me. And as he sat me down, he would look at me very seriously.

"That's how you have to be when you grow up, mijo. Los hombres like Zapata and Villa helped our Raza. They were men of honor and respect. They fought and died for what they believed in."

I would imagine a big man with bullets across his chest with a big sombrero and boots, riding across the mountains of Mexico helping familias and kids. My father also told me stories about my great grandfather, about how he was killed during the Mexican Revolution of 1910. My great grandfather was bringing our familia to safety to the United States. Once he brought them to Texas, he went back to fight for freedom and land that the rich had stolen. He never made it back to Texas. My familia heard rumors and stories that he was killed and thrown off the train that was heading back into the U.S. Some say he died in the battle of Leon, Guanajuato against the Federales.

As a child, it was exciting to think that my great

grandfather was involved in that struggle. I used to tell myself that when I grew up, I was going to be like my great grandfather. Or maybe even like Villa or Zapata. I was confident that I would make a difference.

"Jefito, when I grow up I'm going to be just like them! I'm going to make it better for us," I would say. My father would just smile. How serious could he take me? I was only 5 years old. Now that I think back, I don't think he ever realized that I meant to do what I said. As a child, I didn't need comic book heroes or cartoon heroes. I had real-life heroes, men not afraid to die, men that stood for our Raza, that stopped at nothing to make it better for Mexicans. All of that changed though, once I started first grade in a predominately white school.

"Beaner!" is what I heard as I was getting off the bus at school. I remember looking back at the kids and not even knowing that they were putting me down. I had never heard that word. But by the fourth grade, I knew I was different. I was raised to be proud of being Mexican, but I was never taught to hate any other race. These kids didn't know about Villa or Zapata. They didn't know about the struggles my Raza had gone through. In class, we would study about men like George Washington, Abraham Lincoln, and Christopher Columbus, about the great things they had done. Not once did I hear about my heroes. It made me feel as if my people hadn't done anything great.

In fourth grade, I learned about "American" history in school. But I was learning my own history, from my father, about vatos like Cesar Chavez and Rodolfo "Corky" Gonzales. My father named me after Corky's poem titled 'Yo Soy Joaquín.' I was taught about the Chicano Movement during the '60s when brown berets were worn proudly with fists up high. Raza fighting for their rights. I learned about Cesar Chavez and the UFW march from Delano to Sacramento the capital of Califas. Once I asked my fourth-grade teacher if she could teach the class about Cesar Chavez. She acted as if she didn't know who I was talking about. I never brought it up to her again.

As I entered fifth grade I began to notice other Mexican kids in my school constantly getting picked on. For some reason, Mexicans became an issue to white kids, the same white kids that had been my friends since kindergarten. I too began getting picked on. But what could I do? I was always outnumbered. One day as I was walking to my class after recess, I saw three white boys chasing a young Mexican kid calling him names. No teachers were around because everybody was already walking back to their classrooms. I tried to ignore it but it burned me up inside. One of the boys tripped the Mexican kid and they all began laughing. I just looked down and went to class.

When I went home I talked to my dad about it.

"Papa, were you ever picked on cause you were Mexican when you were young?" He looked at me then sat down. I could tell that he was trying to figure out what to tell me. "Where I grew up, all I knew were Mexicanos," and paused for a second.

"Are you having problems at school mijo?"

"Oh no, I was just asking. I just saw a Mexican kid being bullied around today."

I was lying. I was ashamed to tell him that I was being picked on almost every day.

"Mijo, don't you ever let someone make you feel lower than them because of the color of your skin. I will never tell you to fight! But there is a difference in fighting and defending yourself. Don't ever shame our family blood by ever letting another put you down. Your great grandfather brought his family to Texas hoping we would make a better life for ourselves. And he never let another man put him down."

I agreed and didn't say anything else.

The next day during my lunch recess I walked to the bathroom. It was between a classroom and the cafeteria, so there was hardly any teachers or anyone there. As I was walking out I was stopped at the door by six white kids.

"What are you doing, Beaner? Eating tacos sitting on the toilet?" He looked at his friends to get approval, feeling better as they all laughed. When he saw that they were enjoying it he laughed harder.

"At least he knows where he belongs," said one of the other boys.

Then the tallest of them stepped up and pushed me against the wall. I looked down the hallway hoping a teacher would come. I only saw the Mexican kid from the day before watching.

I pushed him back and said, "Don't you ever push me!"

They were all eating sunflower seeds and they began spitting them at me, pinning me against the bathroom wall. My heart was racing, my hands were sweaty. I was scared. Then I remembered my father and what he told me. My great grandfather would be ashamed of me for not standing my ground. I had sunflower seeds stuck to me with spit. I could hear them laughing. But it felt like a dream where the faster I tried to move, the slower I became. I began to fight the tears I felt coming. They noticed I was scared and laughed at me even more.

"So what are you going to do about it, you little burrito eating wetback."

Then, just as one was going to call me a sissy, I attacked.

"Don't ever call me a Beaner! I'm Mexican!"

I attacked with all my strength as if it were a fight for my life. I punched the taller one right on his mouth. I kicked two other boys and I pushed two more against the wall. I could feel Zapata and Villa fighting along with me, inside of me, in my blood. I felt the rage of my people inside of me, wanting justice for over five hundred years. We had been beaten, raped, killed and mocked. I refused to stand for it any longer.

The first one I hit grabbed me from behind and kicked me. I could hear a teacher running toward us blowing her whistle. I punched one more kid in the stomach and he lost all wind. He fell on his knees, his mouth open, no sound coming out. What seemed like a minute later, he screamed and tears were coming down his cheeks. I laughed as the teacher took us all into the office. I was raging mad, and I didn't even feel where I had been punched and kicked. I knew the spirit of my heroes were flowing in my blood during that fight. After that day, after that fight, I knew in my heart that I would never let anybody put me down or my Raza.

The next day I gathered the only six Mexicans from the fourth and fifth grade during lunch.

"We can't let them push us around anymore. If we stick together and take care of each other nobody will never mess with us again," I said as the kids were sitting close together.

Also with us was the only Black kid in the fifth grade. He too was always getting picked on. Now there was seven of us, and I knew we would never be picked on again. I liked the feeling of power our group gave. We had started a gang.

I guess they get started that easily. I never did let my Jefitos know about the racism at my school. I never let my Jefito's know about my gang either. Every morning we would meet by the sandbox before class started. Then we would meet for recess and lunch.

None of this ever affected my grades though. I would get all As on my report card. I think that's one of the reasons I was never liked by the white kids. They couldn't stand the fact that I was smarter than them. But we were never harassed again. They wouldn't even pick on us when we were by ourselves. They knew that if they did something to one of us, they would have to answer to all of us. The little Mexican kid that saw the whole incident from the bathroom told everybody. He told all the kids that Joaquín had stood up to the white kids. He saw me punch, saw me kick. It had earned me respect from all of the other kids.

Now, I remember the first time my father let me shoot his gun. We took a ride out to the country, and I anticipated every second. He loaded the bullets into a .38 revolver. Then before he let me shoot it, he said that I had to respect the gun. I should never aim at another man unless my familia was threatened. I remember holding the gun and aiming toward an old beer bottle. The rush of hearing the cracking sound as the gun kicked was so powerful that it made my entire body shake. My father would laugh as I missed every single shot. When it was his turn, he aimed with precision, never missing his target.

I didn't mean to go on so long about my childhood, but I felt that it was important to my story. Maybe it will give you a better understanding of me. Everything that happens to us as a child reflects on our adulthood. It's the mold that shapes us into what we become.

2

————————

Six years had passed since that incident in school with the white boys.

"Hey, Loco! What's up for tonight, ese?" yelled out my homeboy Vince from across the hall at school.

"I don't know. Let's just go for a cruise in your primo's ranfla. I heard it's gonna be packed tonight, bro," I yelled back.

"Simón ese, I'll see if he'll lend it to me," as he walked into class.

Vince was my closest camarada since the fourth-grade gang. We both lived on the same block. We never actually kept up with the gang. It was all just kid stuff. But no matter what happened, Vince was always there for me, no matter what the situation. He was dark with a solid build from working out all the time. His hair was always slicked back with *Tres Flores*. He was the kind of vato that loved to joke around, always laughing about something. But when he would get drunk, he would get into fights, especially when he was out with his primo. He lived with his mother and little sister in a small apartment. His father had passed away when he was ten years old. His Jefita would always invite Vince and me to church, hoping someday we would accept her invitation. For one reason or another, we always found an excuse not to go.

We were now in the tenth grade at the only high school in town. That meant that every teenager was there. Chicano's were deep. When I was a kid, the school was surrounded by a mostly white neighborhood. Most of the Mexican's and Blacks lived on the opposite side of town. Now the barrio I grew up in was full of cholos y cholas. We called it Barrio Apache. Even though all the Chicano's were from different barrios and district's in town, we all got along at school. Sometimes we would fight against other vatos from nearby towns, but that was it. After school, all the Raza would hang out at a hamburger stand across the street from the high school, or at the park that was only a block away. During lunch, you would find all the Raza playing handball in the back of the high school against the high walls of the cafeteria. We knew about gang warfare, but that happened in the surrounding towns. We were a small town with a population of about 50,000. I should have realized the disease of gang warfare would seep into our little town soon.

I was now fifteen years old and wearing khakis two sizes too big with the sharpest creases anybody ever saw. I wore a white t-shirt, also baggy, with dark shades for the finishing touch. My hair was combed back, short with a small growing mustache. I was thin with thick arms from push-ups every morning. I wasn't getting good grades anymore. It would be surprising if I even got a grade since I was never in class, to begin with. School became a drag. I hated the teachers, the principal, the classes and the stupid bell that rang. Everybody would hear it and run into class like stupid little sheep. Maybe I just hated discipline and the fact that everybody wanted to tell me what to do. Sometimes Vince and I would ditch class the whole day and just cruise around listening to oldies in his primo's '64 Impala. Vince loved smoking bud. Every single morning he would light one up. But that wasn't for me, chale. It never appealed to me. I always like to stay on my toes, always fully alert.

Finally, it was Friday night as I dialed Vince's number. "Pick me up in 30 minutes ese... I'll be ready," I said to Vince on the phone.

I was at my chante. It was small but my dad owned it. He was always doing something to the house, fixing the yard, painting over old paint. I still needed to finish my creases; they had to be perfect for the cruise that night. I pushed play on my cassette player and let Mary Wells sing to me. There is nada like some tight oldies. Rap y todo is firme, but there's just something about those old songs that make 'em last forever. My little brother walked in. He was five years younger than me. His name was Angel, but we all called him Angelito. I guess because he was the youngest.

"Where are you going Joaquín?" asked my carnalito. "Can I go with you?"

"No, you can't go with me, I'm going out. Your too little to go," I said as I kept ironing. He just sat there and watched me. My carnalito always wanted to spend time with me. He used to always ask if I could walk him to the store for ice cream. I wonder what would go through his head as he stood there and just looked at me. I think he wanted to be like me, always asking me questions about everything I did. Sometimes he would ask me to crease his pants for him. If I had time to crease them, I would. Sometimes our mother would get mad and say, "I don't want another little cholo in the family." I wished I would have spent more time with the little vato. But I was a teenager and the less I was at home the better. I knew that deep down inside he needed me around, but at fifteen years old, I guess I didn't care.

"Your friends here, mijo!" yelled my mother from the kitchen. I quickly changed and was out the door.

"Be careful mijo, don't be home late. You know I can't sleep when your out," she yelled out the door as I was stepping into the ranfla.

"I know, I'll come home early... we're just going for a cruise."

I watched her close the front door as Vince hit the switches and the car dropped to the floor. Then he hit the switch again and raised the front. This ranfla was tight, all white with red pearl, two twelve inch woofers in the trunk and lifted front, back and side to side. I never understood why Vince's primo would let him borrow it. If it was my ranfla I would never let it out of my sight. Vince shook my hand Chicano style and didn't say a word as he put up the volume on the stereo. Old school N.W.A. was bumping loud. Simón, this music was firme, pump anyone up for a fight any day. This was how it was for us every Friday evening. We'd bump the sounds as loud as we could and go straight to the cruise spot. Sometimes we would go to the car wash first and I would help him wash and dry the ranfla. Just as we were cruising for about five minutes, we saw patrol car lights behind us.

"Damn!" said Vince. " I can't believe these pigs. They never leave me alone."

Vince drove another half block and pulled into a gas

station parking lot. The patrol car pulled up right behind us. I could hear the cops as they walked up, handcuffs and keys rattling.

"Let me see your drivers license and registration," asked the cop on Vince's side. The other cop stood on my side, but back toward the rear bumper. I could feel his stare. I knew he was waiting for trouble.

"What am I being pulled over for?" asked Vince as he was taking the license out of his wallet. Then he reached over into the glove compartment to get the registration out.

"Don't worry about why I pulled you over!" said the cop sounding angered.

"Look, officer! I got my license and you know it. You pulled me over a week ago. The ranfla... I mean the car belongs to my cousin."

The cop grabbed the license and registration and walked back to his patrol car. He would run a check on Vince just about every week. It never made sense to me. Every time they pulled him over they acted as if they didn't know who he was. After five minutes of silence between Vince and I, we could hear the officer walking back toward our car. I didn't want to look back because then he would think I was nervous.

"Have you been drinking? Is that marijuana I smell in the car?" asked the officer.

"No we haven't been drinking," I said, "and I don't even smoke marijuana."

"Don't get smart with me you little punk cholo! Get out of the car now!"

I couldn't believe what was happening. We couldn't even have a good time cruising without these pigs constantly bothering us. I slowly opened the door and stepped out of the car. Vince did the same.

"Both of you, stand over here against the car. You wanna get smart with me boy? Let me see your I.D.!"

"I don't have one. Why are you harassing us anyway? Because we're Mexican?" I was so pissed off I could feel my teeth grinding down on each other. Just as I said that two more patrol cars pulled up. Now we had six officers searching the ranfla, looking at me, and looking at Vince.

One of the officers stood two feet from my face and said,

"You got a problem punk?" as he flicks the hat off of my head. I tried to bend down to pick it up and the officer yelled, "Get up! I didn't say you could pick that up yet, did I?"

I stood back up and tried my hardest to hold my anger in. My blood was boiling. If I had a gun I would have killed all of them. There's no way Zapata would ever let Federales treat him like this. He would have pulled out his sword to fight to the death. A crowd of Raza began watching. I could see the helpless look on their faces. Why were these cops acting like this if we had done nothing wrong? Then I realized what was bothering the cops so much. They stopped us hoping Vince's license was suspended or something. Second, when they couldn't find any alcohol or bud, they were pissed, so they were trying to provoke us so that they could bust us for fighting with them. I remembered what my father had told me. The cops and judges wanted all of the Raza on probation or in jail. It was a way to oppress and control us. I mellowed out and let my anger simmer down.

"You got a problem Mexican? You think you're tough?" yelled one of the officers in my face, spraying me with spit.

I looked him straight in his eyes and said,

"No, sir. I got no problem with you."

The pig didn't know how to react, surprised by my answer, not knowing if I was being serious or sarcastic.

"No guns, alcohol or drugs!" yelled the officers that were searching the vehicle. The pigs had no choice but to let us go. I picked my hat up and brushed the dirt off of it. They all slowly walked back to their patrol cars, yelling for everyone to disperse. As Vince and I sat back into the ranfla, one of the patrol cars pulled up next to us.

"It's just a matter of time till you do something wrong. And when you do, you better believe I'm going to be there," said the officer on the passenger side. Then he smiled sarcastically and drove off.

We cruised on for ten minutes without either of us saying a word. I felt so humiliated for letting the pig bully us like that and hitting the hat off my head. Cruising wasn't much fun after that, so we just headed back to the barrio. Vince dropped me off at home. I went straight to bed. I wanted to crash out and forget the whole night.

The next day everyone at school was talking about a new gang in town that was taking over, and anyone that wouldn't join them would be beaten. They were called Varrio Side Locos or VSL. They were from the opposite side of town, so I didn't even think much about it. I was from Barrio Apache, far from VSL. During the next few weeks, I kept hearing about VSL jumping vatos at the park, at the school and even at the hamburger stand. I was never really around because Vince and I would just go out of town every day during school and cruise other high schools. I couldn't figure out why anybody would want to start a gang in such a small town. We'd always gotten along with all of the Raza, so I never saw the need for a gang-

One Saturday afternoon I was sitting outside listening to the radio. I heard tires screeching as Vince turned the corner and pulled into my driveway. I knew something was wrong.

He wasn't driving his primo's ranfla. He had an old cutlass, painted with grey primer. He jumped out of the car with his shirt ripped and blood coming from his mouth.

"Hey bro, then vatos jumped me at the car wash!" he said.

I already knew who he was talking about. I didn't have to ask.

"For what ese, what were you doing?" I asked not understanding why anybody would jump my camarada, my homie since we were kids.

"They said I was in their barrio and that I didn't belong there. I've lived in this town and in this barrio all my life, ese! I'm not going to let anyone tell me I can't be here. They tried surrounding me so I hit the closest vato to me. Then I got hit on the side of my jaw. They started kicking me! Then I jumped into my ranfla cause I knew I couldn't fight all of them. They even broke my side window trying to punch me as I drove off. Chale with that, vato! If that's how they want to play, then I can play right back!"

All of a sudden I felt my blood rise with hate. I loved this homie, and here he was standing in front of me bleeding. I didn't even think about the consequences as I ran into my room and grabbed my wooden baseball bat. It was hidden under my bed in case I ever needed it. There was no hesitation as I jumped into the ranfla.

"Let's go!" I said as Vince was getting back into the car. He was spitting blood from the mouth. He headed straight to the car wash. It felt like hours to get there. All I kept thinking about was hurting these vatos, these punks. I couldn't believe they had the nerve to hit Vince up. He was born in this town. I didn't want to get involved with these vatos from VSL, but Vince was my camarada. Any assault on him was an assault on me.

"Pull over around the back of the car wash. Just go through the alley. We'll walk behind the building and catch them vatos slipping," I said to Vince. We parked across a small side street and quickly walked behind the old red brick building next to the car wash. I could feel my heart pounding crazy. I was surprised that Vince couldn't hear my heartbeats. Vince was right behind me. He wore a pair of brass knuckles he got from his tio a while back. He kept them stashed in his glove compartment. I looked around the building and saw three vatos from VSL. They were only about four feet from me. I could smell bud, so I knew they were blazing. I could hear them laughing about what they had done to Vince.

I ran toward the closest vato and said, "You wanna try to jump vatos when they're by themselves ese!" and I took my first swing with the bat. I felt the impact through my whole body as I hit him on his shoulder and back. His eyes showed terror as I hit him over and over on his body. Vince grabbed the second vato and hit him with the brass knuckles straight in the face two times before the fool knew what hit 'em. I was already on the third vato beating him with my bat and kicking him in the head. The first vato I hit was still on the ground holding his face, hoping I wouldn't hit him again.

"Don't ever try to jump me again, chavalas! This is our town, and we go where we want!" yelled Vince as he kept punching the vato in the head and face. Blood was everywhere, on his knuckles and shirt. But this time it wasn't Vince's blood.

"¡Ya, no mas! Let's go vato, before the pigs get here," I said as I gave the first vato I hit one last solid kick in the jaw. Vince wouldn't stop punching the vato. It was as if he was in a trance. I could hear the vato whimpering. He was curled up as Vince stood over him. I had to pull Vince away and practically pull him back to the car. I could already see a crowd gathering so I figured it was just a matter of minutes before cops would be all over the car wash. We jumped into the ranfla and headed straight to my chante.

———

3

"What's going to happen now?" asked Vince as he cleaned the blood from his hands and arms. I just sat there, realizing that we had just started a war, a war we had no chance of winning. VSL had at least thirty members in their gang, and that wasn't counting all their older brothers, cousins and vatos that just hung around trying to get into the gang. I knew we had to do something but didn't know what.

"I guess all we can do is wait to see what happens. We just gotta stay trucha from now on," I said as I looked out of my bedroom window. I was just waiting for carloads of vatos to pull up into the driveway with bats, or worse, with cuetes. We stayed up almost all night and to our surprise, nobody from VSL ever drove by my house that night.

The next morning as I woke up, I couldn't believe what had happened the night before. I got up and took a quick shower. I ironed real quick, not really trying to get perfect creases this time. I just wasn't in the mood for it. All of the great men that died for the Raza. All the thousands of lives that were forever ended. Villa, Zapata, and soldados that bled the ground. What was it all for? So vatos could go around beating each other up? Cops were always harassing Chicanos. I had never shoplifted, tagged on walls or got into fights. I had no criminal record whatsoever, but I was still treated like a criminal.

My parents were eating my favorite breakfast, chorizo mixed with papas.

"How are you doing mijo?" asked my father as he noticed my anxiety.

"I'm doing good. Just going to school," I replied. I didn't want to worry them about what had happened.

"Are you sure?" asked my father concerned.

"Yeah, I'm ok, I just stayed up late last night," I answered.

No matter what problems I had, it always felt good to sit with my parents. I don't know how my father kept us together, even through the bad times. We didn't always have money but I can honestly say I never had to go hungry. We always had a roof over our head and a meal on our table. I sat and ate with them feeling better, knowing that they would always be there for me. I served myself a second serving and finished it quickly. Then I kissed my mother on the cheek and left.

I decided to walk toward the corner store that was only two blocks away, thinking nothing would happen. When I got there I saw some homeboys next to the payphones.

"Hey Loco, come over here, ese," said Chuey as he hung up the phone. I lived in the Barrio Apache, so I had a lot of vatos grow up with me. We would never hang around as a gang together because like I said, everybody got along in town. Chuey was a couple years older than me and he had done tiempo in C.Y.A. for breaking into a gun shop. He had tattoos on his back, neck, chest, and stomach. The most recognizable was Apache in Old English across his stomach.

I walked over to him as we gave each other a Chicano handshake.

"What happened yesterday homie? I heard about a fight from some jaina this morning," said Chuey.

Tobo and Big Ed also walked up to shake my hand. These three vatos were always together. I'd known all of them since I was a kid.

"How did you know about that?" I asked, surprised that it had gotten around already.

"Everybody's talking about it. You vatos went off on them fools, huh? Don't trip though, bro... we got your back."

I didn't expect him to say that, even though we were all from the same barrio.

Big Ed was a big vato. He sold all the bud in Barrio Apache. He was the vato that always had feria in his wallet. Tobo was the crazy one, the one that would fight dirty to win. One time he got arrested for fighting with a cop. The story was that the cop called him a wetback. It took four cops to finally cuff him. Then they beat the living crap out of him. Up until this point, these vatos were just guys I grew up with from around the block, and I felt better being at the store with them around. I felt good to know that somebody was on our side. Yet I knew that this wasn't the end of it, but the beginning.

Two days had passed without a single incident. I actually thought that everything was just going to blow over. So after school Vince and I decided to cruise by the high school. Everybody was getting out and we wanted to see some Jainas. It was all firme at that point. I saw a homegirl I knew, so I called her over to the ranfla. Just as she walked up to my side of the car, I heard a yell, "VSL rifa!"

I turned around and couldn't believe it. We got caught slipping and they were surrounding us. I tried to analyze the situation. They had two ranflas in front of us and behind us, locking us in. On one side was a wall, and on the other side some cars. The first vato to get out of the ranfla was the one Vince had hit with the brass knuckles.

"Let's see how you like it," said the vato, as he stepped out with a baseball bat walking towards me. I looked around again and knew that there was no way we were going to get out of this situation. I counted nine cholos with them. Just as they were all stepping out of their ranflas I heard a police siren.

"What's going on!" yelled the cop as he quickly stepped out of his vehicle, hand on his stick.

"Nothing man, nothing," said one of the VSL vatos. They all quickly got back into their cars and drove off. Vince started his ranfla and we also drove off before the cops decided to mess with us again. I'm not going to lie. I was glad the pigs pulled up. Vince and I were down to fight, but I knew that this time they would have killed us. As bad as we beat up their homeboys the other day, I knew they wanted revenge.

"Look ese, they're waiting to see which way we're going," I said as I saw both cars a few blocks away.

"Just jam back to Barrio Apache... at least we got a better chance to find some homeboys to back us up."

"Chale! I'm going to my tio's chante downtown. He has a shotgun. I'm going to kill them fools!"

I didn't know what to think. I just knew that we were getting deeper and deeper into this mess. Vince punched the gas and went through a red light. The cars following close behind did the same and started gaining on us. We turned a sharp corner into an alley and through a parking lot. Just as we turned into his uncle's driveway the other vatos pulled up behind us. Vince ran into the front door of his uncle's house. There was no way of turning this situation around, so I figured the hell with it. I jumped out from my seat and yelled, "You got a problem? Let's go at it one on one!"

I knew they weren't going for it. They rushed me from all sides as I tried my hardest to punch my way out of it. I was getting kicked, punched and pushed when I heard the shots.

Boom! Boom! Boom!

I could hear the pellets fall everywhere as the buckshot came down. They stopped kicking me and looked up as Vince stood on his uncle's porch with a sawed-off twelve gauge shotgun shooting into the air.

"Get up out of here! Don't you ever try to run up on me!" said Vince as he now aimed the shotgun toward them. I could see the rage in his face.

"I'll blast every single one of you chavalas!"

They all slowly stepped back and got into their ranflas. I wasn't sure what to expect. I didn't know if they had any cuetes or not.

"We'll get you punks. You better watch your back!" yelled one of the vatos from his passenger side window.

They hit the gas and peeled off, throwing gang signs out of the window. We quickly locked up Vince's ranfla and ran into the house. Vince hid the twelve gauge in the garage under a stack of old clothes. Then we quickly ran out of the back door toward the alley. We figured the cops would be coming anytime. There was an old pizza place a block away from the alley. It had an arcade upstairs where a lot of vatos hung out and played video games. It was always dark with an old jukebox. We made it just in time because as we walked upstairs, we heard cop sirens pass by. Inside, there were vatos playing pool and games. We blended in. The police sirens kept passing down the street. We both looked at each other and tried ignoring the fact that the cops were after us. VSL was after us. I guess the whole world is after us.

That night I laid in bed thinking about how everything had escalated from one small incident into a big one. Never did I think that I would be in this situation. Vince and I weren't new to gangbanging, but we never had to fight against vatos from our own town. I had a tio that was killed in the late fifties. He lived in Coolidge, a small town in Arizona. It was over a dice game. My father would tell me stories about his brother. He would tell me that he was a hardcore pachuco. He wouldn't even carry a knife. He carried a big razor blade, ready to cut any vato across the stomach. Back then they wouldn't try to stab you, they would slice you. It was a harder cut to heal, especially when your intestines were hanging out. My familia bloodline was involved in this Vida Loca even back then in those times. Tambien during the 70's, my father's primo was killed in Califas. Dying and murder was just a fact of life, whether we vatos liked it or not.

In our town the veteranos were proud of the fact that we all got along, so I wondered how they felt about our situation. I couldn't stop thinking about what was going to happen. It would either blow over or get worse, and I just knew that there was no way it would simply blow over.

That night I dreamed about snakes. No matter which way I turned I saw snakes crawling over each other. I couldn't get away. They seemed to fall from the sky. And each time I woke up covered with sweat, I would toss and turn, only to dream again of snakes.

I woke up to the sound of oldies when my alarm went off. I didn't want to wake up. Chale, just to live another stressful day. I slowly got up and ironed my brown Dickies and black Pendleton. Taking a slow shower, dreading the fact of going to school. I looked into the mirror and made sure my hair was combed perfectly back. I put on my *pano* across the forehead. I heard Vince pull into my driveway as I was eating breakfast.

"Vince is outside," said my mother as she watered the plants outside.

"Ok" I answered as I shoved the rest of the food into my mouth. I grabbed my pocket knife from the dresser in my room and walked out. Vince had his primo's '64. He was rolling a joint as I sat in the car.

"This is some good bud, homie. Big Ed must have a firme connect," said Vince as he finished rolling the joint.

I didn't say anything. I had never been into yesca. I was surprised that Vince was acting as if nothing was going on. He started the car and hit the switches and the car rose. We cruised straight to the high school. I actually felt like going to class today. But before we parked Vince decided to take a cruise around the school because it gave us a chance to see some of the homies and jainas. Just as we were about to park, I could see Chuey running toward us.

"It's on vato! It's on!" yelled Chuey as he reached us. I was confused because I knew that Chuey didn't go to school. I figured the reason Chuey was even at the school was that sometimes he walked his lady.

"What are you talking about, bro?" asked Vince as he was getting out of the '64.

"Then chavalas from VSL just jumped me," said Chuey.

Now I looked at him and I noticed his face was scuffed up. His shirt was dirty and he had blood on his fists. Just then Big

Ed pulled up with a carload of vatos from Barrio Apache. Big Ed jumped out from his car and ran toward Chuey to make sure he was ok. I had never seen Big Ed so pissed off before. I could see the hate in his eyes. He was acting as if he was the one who got jumped. I know the feeling of having a good homeboy get hurt and you're not there to back him up.

Big Ed looked toward us and said: "Let's go."

Chuey jumped into Big Ed's car. Vince didn't say a word as he sat back into his ranfla. I knew it was time to ride. We followed Big Ed toward the parking lot on the other side of the school. As we turned toward the parking lot on the other side of the school I saw them. There were about fifteen vatos from VSL mean mugging us like they wanted to kill us. With no hesitation, Big Ed jumped out of his ranfla and knocked the biggest vato out. He hit that vato so hard I could hear the solid impact from where I was standing.

"Yeah! Puro Barrio Apache!" yelled Big Ed as he hit another vato twice in the face.

It seemed like time stopped as everyone just stood and watched in shock. Then as everyone realized what was happening, it started. Every single vato began throwing punches, kicks, garbage cans and anything else that could be thrown. I felt a hit from behind my head. I could feel warm blood running down my neck. I felt myself begin to fall when a homeboy helped me up. I shook it off and ran into the fighting crowd. It was the worst fight I had ever seen in my whole life. We had about eight homies with us. VSL had about fifteen vatos with them. Vatos were getting hit and kicked all around me. I saw Big Ed get hit with a stick. I saw Vince kicking a vato in the mouth. Before I knew it, gente from the school began jumping into the fight. I saw vatos and jainas boxing. Some were fighting with us, some were fighting against us. I figured it was about thirty-five people throwing blows. I saw one vato from VSL staggering next to me. I didn't hesitate to hit him right on the side of his head with all my strength. It felt like slow motion when I saw him fall. I could hear some jainas screaming for us to stop.

"Let's go!" yelled Big Ed as he backed up from the fight. His shirt was ripped off and hanging from his waist. I could see Tobo getting kicked on the ground as four vatos from VSL surrounded him. Vince ran toward them and kicked one of the vatos in the mouth. It looked like an explosion of blood. I ran over to back up Vince and Tobo. People were running around all crazy not knowing where to go. I pushed a vato away from Tobo and began choking him. I wanted to kill this vato. I wanted to see him take his last breath. He was trying to pull my hands away with all of his strength. I could feel him getting weak. I felt someone tugging at me. I turned around and it was Vince with blood running down his face. Teachers were trying to break the fight up. I let the vato go as he turned over throwing up and coughing.

"I just called the cops!" yelled the white math teacher as he tried pulling two vatos apart. They were wrestling on the floor. I saw someone from VSL run behind the teacher and hit him in the back of the head. The teacher fell as some of the vatos began kicking the teacher. I could hear the teacher crying in pain. I hate that racist teacher anyways, I thought to myself. We ran back toward our ranflas and everybody was running in different directions. Some of the homies were carrying Tobo to Big Ed's car. VSL began running into the school before the cops got there. They had all walked to school so they had no form of getting away. Vince peeled out and followed behind Big Ed.

4

"Meet at my chante," yelled Big Ed from his window as we drove toward Barrio Apache. We could hear police sirens coming closer as we took a side street. I was sweating with adrenaline just knowing that the cops were going to find us. I looked back toward the main street and saw all the police cars pass by. They were heading toward the high school.

"They just passed us by," I said. We were packed seven deep. All vatos from Barrio Apache, vatos I knew growing up, some younger some older.

As we drove up to Big Ed's chante I counted four parked cars in front of his house. Big Ed signaled for us to go inside quickly from his bedroom window. We all got out of the ranfla and quickly went into his pad. Big Ed's Jefitos were both at work and his sister went to college. The second I walked in I could see clouds of marijuana smoke. The smell of skunk bud hit me as I inhaled the air. As I walked into the back room everybody gave me hugs and Chicano handshakes. It seemed as if this gente had been here for hours, but they were involved in the fight at the school. Vatos were throwing punches into the air excitedly as they told each other about who they had hit. We even had girls in the house talking about how many vatos they had fought. Vince asked Big Ed for a towel so he could wipe the blood from his face. I could see Tobo laying down on an old mattress holding his leg. It looked really bad. I walked toward him and kneeled down. I asked, "Are you ok?"

"Simón ese, I'm ok. I think it's only bruised and cut," he answered.

"Are you sure it's not broken?" I asked with rap music playing loud above our voices.

"I'll be firme. I can still walk," he answered. "It's going to take more than some punks from VSL to keep me down, ese," as he smiled. I stood back up as I gripped his shoulder. I shook his hand as if we had just won a deadly battle.

One of the homeboys named Spider ran in and said "The cops are driving around outside! Everybody be quiet."

Everybody instantly stopped talking as Big Ed turned his radio off. He walked to the front of his house to investigate whether the cops were just driving around or stopping there. They drove by the house and then drove off. They had no idea we had at least thirty heads in the house.

"I'm sick of them fools from VSL! Let's go to their hangout and jump anybody we see," exclaimed Spider.

"Hell no, ese. Let's kill one of them fools, shoot up their familia and everything," yelled a youngster named Macho. I couldn't believe it. We got into a fist fight and now these vatos wanted to go around shooting everybody. I never realized how many homies I had from Barrio Apache, and these homies weren't everyone. Then everybody started talking at once about what to do about VSL. As they were talking, I was reminded of the little fifth-grade gang.

I stood up and said "Who is really down for this? Everybody here just got into one fight, but are you really ready for the long run? Believe me, VSL is not going to stop now. If anything, we just pissed them off worse. Simón, we all talk big and bad now because we got a gang of homies here. Everybody's all pumped up to fight. But what's going to happen when you're alone at a gas station, or with your little sisters or brothers at the park. Or when you're with you moms or abuelas. Are you really ready to be down to the fullest, or are you just half-stepping into something you know nothing about? Simón, I'm tired of them vatos tambien. And I'm already involved because of what Vince and I did at the car wash. Most of you don't have to be involved. Just go back to school and forget about today. We appreciated that you helped us but I don't want the Apache gang to be the reason for your downfall. If you want to leave, then go ahead. Nobody here will think any less of you."

I stopped talking and slowly looked around the room. I couldn't believe the confidence I felt talking in front of all this gente. But it felt good. I felt the same power I felt when I had the fifth-grade gang. The same rage and power in my sangre. Once again Zapata and Villa came alive in me. I pictured Emiliano Zapata making a speech in front of thousands of peasants as they rode into battle. I could envision Villa riding his black horse with his soldados behind him, shotguns in hand. It must have been a beautiful yet terrible thing to experience, fighting along fellow men and women for land.

To my amazement, nobody left. I could see that everybody was thinking and letting my words sink in. That's when I knew that nobody was going to leave. Everybody was sick and tired of VSL going around beating on people. No one leaving, I figured that I had to keep talking. I was hoping someone else would get up and talk, but they didn't. It was obviously up to me. I was always the one to make the first move. All the decisions were always on my shoulders. My father taught me to be a leader, not a follower. He taught me to think for myself, and to never say anything without thinking about it first.

"If they want to start a stupid gang within our town and start banging VSL, then I see no problem if we bang BARRIO APACHE! We are the only barrio in town not bowing down to them punks. From now on, any vatos that aren't from Apache we got to jam them up," I said hitting my fist for exclamation.

"We got to let them chavalas know that they can't come into Barrio Apache. We got to protect ourselves and our hood from them vatos, cause nobody else will."

I could tell that the homies were getting excited. My blood was rushing within me. I refused to let them VSL vatos take our town over. We now had thirty members in our small click. Not bad for the first day. We all made promises to each other that we would back up Barrio Apache with all of our hearts, con todo el corazon.

For the rest of the day, everybody just kicked it. The radio went back on and the weed was smoked once again, filling the house with thick smoke. Gangs are started that easily. I never thought the day would come where I would hate my own Raza. Here I was wanting to kill other Chicanos from another gang. To think, all my father had taught me didn't matter in the real world. And although my heroes were Villa and Zapata, they were history. Nobody cared about the struggle anymore. Nobody cared if Zapata fought for the poor. It just didn't matter anymore. Everything now was just spoils of war. I actually believed I was going to do something great for my people. Now I knew that it was all lost, the causa, the revolution, even the pride, and my gente.

Two months had passed and things were worse with each day. Now there were at least sixty Apache members in the gang, not counting the youngsters trying to get into the clicka. Everything was tense all over town as fights broke out at the high school, local parks and fast food places. Vatos and jainas were getting suspended and expelled from school all of the time. Every single Chicano in town felt as if they had to pick a side for their safety.

VSL was also growing in numbers so much that I didn't recognize all of their faces anymore. Tobo was on crutches for a month because of his damaged leg from the big fight at the school. My parents knew that something was going on with me. They constantly asked me why I was so quiet. They said I was acting like a different person.

I knew I was different. But Vince was even more loco. I saw Vince lose all fear of death. I slowly saw him turn into a cold-blooded gang banger almost overnight. I wondered if I had also changed. I wasn't sure. But maybe I had and I couldn't tell. Everything had happened so quickly that I still didn't know how to feel. One day everybody in town got along and the next we had to watch our back every time we went out. My town was small with only four main streets. No matter where I went I would see VSL. I couldn't even go grocery shopping with my mother anymore. I was bound to see one of them chavalas and a fight would break out.

Every time something would go down in the Barrio the homeboys would come to me. They always wanted my opinion about every single situation. Everything was getting out of control, and there was no way for me to stop it. I would never leave because my homeboys needed me. So that's how I became the leader of a gang. I didn't want to lead. I didn't ask for the job. But deep down inside my heart, I knew I loved the power, even though I never admitted it to anyone else.

The homeboys would drive all over town and tag the walls, writing Barrio Apache with spray cans. They would cross out anyone else that had written on the wall. Sometimes the other gang would try to retaliate and come into Barrio Apache to tag our walls with their gang name. It was a major disrespect for anybody to come into our barrio and cross our names out. All we had was our homeboys and neighborhood. When anyone drove onto our streets, they knew it was Apache territory. Sometimes they got away with it, and sometimes they didn't. I guess that was the risk of it all. Big Ed always complained of the fights, saying it messed up his bud slanging. Chuey got locked up for the big fight at the school parking lot. A teacher recognized him and called the cops on him. They went to his house and picked him up. It didn't matter. He was going to be out after doing two and a half months. The everyday stress was finally weighing on me. I never thought that gangbanging could be so tiresome. All I wanted to do was rest. It felt as if I was drowning or being crushed. But who could I tell? I didn't have anyone to lean on. I couldn't ever see an end to any of it.

One night, Vince and his primo pulled up to Burger King for some food. I decided to kick it with a jaina at my chante, so I didn't go with them. They were always being trucha, but I guess they didn't see the vatos from VSL parked across the lot. Vince had smoked some green skunk and was feeling good. As he stepped out of his ranfla he noticed some jainas next to a payphone. Vince's primo had been drinking too, so he was feeling buzzed. Vince noticed the jainas giggling and flirting with him. So he walked up to them. They all had firme smiles and were looking good.

"¿Qué onda? Where's the party at?" asked Vince as he lit a cigarette. He heard footsteps and sensed something was wrong. As he turned around he felt a hit below his ribs. He tried to throw a punch and noticed blood coming out his side. The jainas started screaming as he lifted his shirt and saw a knife stab. Blood was spraying out as the vato stabbed him again. Vince's primo was being jumped by three vatos next to his car. They had pulled him out through his window. Another vato pushed Vince down as he felt his knees give way, weakened. He tried to fight but didn't have the strength to swing. All he could do was to try and block the vato from stabbing him as he felt the knife cutting his arms and hands. He felt each stab wound rip his flesh. He fought to keep his eyes open; he didn't want to die.

"Yeah, fool! Now, what punk? VSL rifamos! And don't you ever forget it!" yelled the vato as he stabbed Vince in the gut one more time. Blood was coming out of Vince's mouth as he tried to breath. I wonder what went through Vince's mind at that moment. What did he feel? Did he see his little sister or his Jefito? Or did he see his mother looking down at him asking why, as she screamed and cried? I wonder if his mother woke up with tears running down her face. Little did she know her son was dying. Did he feel scared, hate or love? Or did he just feel the will to live, to breath just one more day? As the punks ran off, his primo crawled to where Vince was laying. Vince's primo could hear one of the jainas call the paramedics. Vince gasped for air as he stared at his primo. He was begging for help as he laid soaked in blood. One single tear came down his eye and that was that. That was the way my camarada died, my brother, my homie.

The funeral was full of cholos, cholas and Vince's familia. Some vatos wore black t-shirts with R.I.P and Vince's name in Old English lettering. It was a sign of respect from the gang. His mother and grandparents were there, along with familia from different states. They all cried silently. Patrol cars were driving by every few minutes making sure there was no trouble. I didn't know what to feel. I had lost a brother. I felt so much hate, like cancer that's slowly eating away at me inside. I never meant for all this to go this far. I wanted it to stop. I was firme with fighting, and tagging up on walls. But this was something permanent. Nothing was going to bring Vince back.

Every single gang member was being rounded up by the cops. We couldn't be in groups of three homies or more. The cops were crashing down hard on the barrios. An employee from Burger King snitched and described who the killer was. Cops found the vato that stabbed Vince a few towns away and brought him back to town. They put him into the county jail with the general population. Come to find out he wasn't even from VSL. He was from a city nearby and had a cousin in VSL. After two days in jail, cops found him stabbed to death in the showers. We never knew who did it. The cops thought that we had something to do with it, but we didn't have anybody in the county jail at the time. Chuey was there, but he was in lockdown. Some say it was a big prison gang that did the hit. Vince had a tio serving 20 years for murdering a vato in a drug deal. He was a shot caller and could have had anybody killed at any time.

A few weeks passed as I sat in my homeboy's garage. The chante belonged to a veterano that had just been released from the pen. He was a tattoo artist. We all called him Vete but his name was Francisco. I took my shirt off. Big Ed, Tobo and Chuey sat there as I was getting ready to get my first tattoo. I wanted Apache across my stomach in Old English writing. The homeboys told each other jokes as I quietly sat there. I didn't feel like joking. Matter of fact, I didn't feel anything.

"Go ahead ese, might as well start now," I said to Vete as he sharpened the needle made from a guitar string.

"Do you want it shaded in, or just shaded along the top and bottom of the letters?"

"I want it all shaded in homeboy. Let everyone know without a doubt that I'm from Apache," I answered as I clenched my teeth. I couldn't help but think of my homeboy laying in a box buried six feet deep. Revenge for Vince was mine. He was my carnal that put his vida down for Barrio Apache. I hated VSL more than ever. I would never stop until everyone from VSL was dead. I wondered if it would have happened differently if I had been there. Why hadn't I kicked it with him instead of a jaina? I tightened my fists as Vete started his work. I could feel the needle pinching my skin as oldies played. I closed my eyes as I felt a monster building up inside of me. Would I die in the calles like Vince? I didn't know and I didn't care.

"How much feria for that cuete homes?" I asked the vato. I drove to a city to buy a throwaway gun. He was a friend of my cousin. I now had a nice '65 Chevy with the original gold paint still on it. The primo I grew up with was with me. His name was Alfredo and he had moved to town because it got too hot for him in his barrio. He stabbed two vatos from a barrio he was fighting with. His Jefita made him move in with us, thinking it was much calmer in our smaller town. As far as I was concerned it was worse. At least he lived in a bigger city. You didn't necessarily see your enemies every time you turned a corner like in this town.

"Just give me a hundred dollars for it. It ain't got no bodies on it," said the vato.

I counted the money and put the cuete under my seat. I handed him the bills as he shook my hand. It was a .38 Special revolver. Not bad for a first cuete. I had just turned eighteen two months ago. My primo Alfredo was two years older than me. He grew up in the projects so this gangbanging vida was far from new to him. A year had passed since the day Vince was buried.

But things were really getting out of hand now. Vatos were constantly getting harassed by cops because their car would have three or four vatos in it. Cops would search the ranflas we were in looking for knives and guns. There were high school counselors always trying to preach to us against barrio warfare. My homeboys were constantly going in and out of jail. Some of the homies were even snorting coke or rolling joints with coke mixed into it. Little youngsters from my barrio were putting in work and claiming Apache, too. I had kids as young as ten asking me if they could be in our gang. Chale con eso. I didn't want that kind of responsibility. I didn't want any little kids around me. I knew I was in too deep with no turning back. I was going to die for the choices I made. I didn't want to drag any kids into this crazy lifestyle. The youngsters didn't listen to me anyway, and they just started their own gang.

I had grown and forgot anything my dad had ever taught me. To think that I actually wanted to grow up to help my Raza. My father hardly talked to me now. I could tell he was ashamed of me. But no matter what I went through I still had respect for my parents. Pero besides that, I only had love for my homeboys, my Barrio. If you weren't from Barrio Apache, then you were my enemy. This is our Barrio and I swore to God, on the day I saw Vince lowered, that I would die for Apache. I would back it up till my last dying breath.

On the way back to town after buying the cuete Alfredo my cousin said, "Let's go to the park primo."

"Orale, but do me a favor, ese. Load my cuete," I answered as I exited the freeway and headed straight to my Barrio park. The park had a giant concrete dead end towards the middle of it. Everybody would cruise in and park along the sides. All the older homies from Apache would go almost every weekend to barbecue. It had small hills throughout the park with lots of old twisted trees for shade.

"What's up?" said Chuey as we pulled up to park. I shook his hand as I got out of the car. He had just been released from jail for an assault a few months back. It felt good to see him out and free.

"Nada homie," I answered as I walked with him to where the homeboys were standing. I could smell bud as I walked closer to the park benches.

"¿Qué onda?" yelled one of the older vatos from the hood.

"Nada, nomas another day," I said as I shook everybody's hand and sat down.

Big Ed, Tobo, Chuey, Spider, and Dragon were all talking about a fight they had gotten into the night before. It wasn't too often that they were all out of jail and kicking back at the same time. Luckily I hadn't been caught for anything. I was the only vato that hadn't done any time yet. My primo Alfredo would put in work for Apache so he was quickly accepted as one of the homies. Plus, he was related to me. It was a firme day, puro oldies, rap and carne cooking on the grill.

As the sun began to set some of the older homies began packing up. They had their kids and ladies with them. They knew how rowdy it got on some nights. I didn't trip. I had a brand new cuete ready to put a bullet into a chavala. Some of the homies were passing out beers and rolling joints when suddenly we saw two cars pull into the park. We knew exactly who it was.

"Everybody stay trucha," said Spider as he stood closest to the parking lot.

Eight vatos from VSL jumped out of their ranflas. Barely waiting for their cars to stop, Spider walked up to them.

"You want some pleito?" he asked as he swung and missed. Two vatos jumped on him as we all ran towards them. I ran straight towards Spider and punched one of the vatos right before he was going to kick him in the head. I felt metal at the side of my head and heard the click of a trigger being pulled back. I stopped fighting and stood up.

"Now you ain't so bad chavala. I could kill you right now... punk."

No one moved as everyone waited for the gun to blow my face to pieces. I felt my heart drop. I knew I was going to die. I thought of my mother and father. Everything went silent for me. It was like watching a silent film, a film of bit and pieces of my life. I could see my father telling me a story, I could see when Vince and I would ditch school. I could see my mother making breakfast and smiling as she sat with me. Then I could only feel the cold metal against my temple. I began to think of Vince and how he died. I wanted to yell 'do it, do it if you got heart.' Then in an instant, I was no longer scared to die. Something in me wanted to die. Once, a veterano told me that a man that's scared to die will never really live.

"Pull the trigger, ese, if you got heart," I said with hate in my voice. But I could see the weakness in his eyes. I glanced at Spider who was trying to get up. I could see blood running down his nose and mouth. I felt raging mad with anger like I wanted to rip my chest open. I was so sick of everything. I saw the vato look toward his homeboys. They were all in shock, not knowing if he was going to do it or not. I could see the fear in their eyes as the tension thickened. And in one quick second, as he turned toward his homeboys, I grabbed the barrel. I aimed it up as we wrestled for the gun. He pulled the trigger as it shot into the air. My ears were ringing as I smelled burning gun powder. Punches were once again being thrown. Then another shot hit the light towering over. Pieces of glass came down on us. Darkness covered us with no moon in sight. His pistol dropped as I hit him in the face. He reached down to grab it, but I quickly kicked him with all of my strength. My shoe hit his nose as blood began pouring. I looked around and everybody was fighting. I could hear someone yelling that they had been stabbed. I turned around and saw Dragon holding his lower chest. Blood was coming out of his mouth as he fell on his knees.

I stepped back and pulled out my cuete. The vato I had kicked was still trying to reach for his gun on the cement. I quickly pulled the hammer back and aimed. I felt like throwing up. I knew that I was going to destroy this man in a split second. I thought about my father and Villa. I wondered how Zapata felt when he shot his first Federal. Did he feel any remorse knowing the Federal was also a Mexican? Is this what my life was going to be? I felt angry at myself for feeling any kind remorse for this vato. I snapped out of it as I heard the loud gunshot. I looked down and saw the vato staring at me in disbelief. He was holding his chest as blood poured out. I put the cuete into my pocket and ran to the other side of the fight. I could hear him yelling for help. I ran toward the restrooms and nervously cleaned my gun with my shirt. I could still hear the fighting as I emptied all of the bullets.

I tossed the gun into a nearby field. As I ran back I could see them carrying the vato into the car. My homeboys were running through the park carrying Dragon. Alfredo was standing next to my car looking for me.

"Where did you go, ese!" yelled Alfredo. He was the only person that knew I had a gun.

"I tossed the cuete in the field," I said as I started up the car and peeled out. I headed straight for the freeway. I had to get as far away from this fight as possible. I didn't say anything more to Alfredo. I lowered my window and let the cool night air in. I wondered if I had killed him. Was he begging for his life as Vince did? Why was I so concerned about this vato? I hated all them fools from VSL. It was something that had to be done. I did it for my barrio. I did it for Vince.

5

———

I figured I had gotten away from the shooting at the park. Nobody knew I had a cuete that night. Not even my own homeboys. They figured I had done it, but they never asked me. The vato I shot didn't die, but he never told the pigs anything. The shooting was in the newspaper the next day. It said that there were no witnesses to the shooting. It was all over town that VSL wanted to kill me. They knew exactly who did the shooting. I knew that he wanted revenge himself. I didn't care. Nothing mattered either way. I had shot him in the chest just missing his heart. Too bad he didn't die, I thought to myself. I wanted them punks to know how it felt. I wanted them to feel the pain I felt when Vince was killed. I wanted that punks familia to cry just like Vince's familia cried. Let them know how it feels to lose a camarada.

I had a homeboy we called Crow who'd grown up with me since I was five. He was two years younger than me. He moved to Mexico right before all of the trouble Vince and

I got into. Because his abuelo was dying, his entire familia moved down there. His abuelo passed away a few months later. So Crow didn't want to live in Mexico anymore. Big Ed told him to come back and live with him. He had no idea it had gotten this bad. He learned real quick.

"I'm going to drop you off at Big Ed's, ese. It was good to see you homie," I said as I pulled into Big Ed's driveway.

"Simón, bro. It feels good to be back in my town," answered Crow. He was dark and heavyset with a small thin mustache. He was always the type of homie to do anything for you. He reminded me of Vince.

"I can't believe Vince is gone," he said. "I didn't even know he got killed, man. I'm sorry, I know how tight you vatos were."

"Yeah, but he's gone now. I can't be trippin' on the past," I said wanting to change the subject. I could feel my fists tighten as anger began building up inside me, like a volcano ready to erupt.

Crow noticed my uneasiness as he quickly changed the subject.

"Let's kick it tomorrow vato. We'll go play some pool or something," said Crow as he shook my hand and stepped out of the car.

"Sounds firme," I said as I nodded my head.

I put the ranfla in reverse and pulled back into the street. As I was leaving and turning on my headlights I noticed something. I began to drive forward when I saw silhouettes in the dark. I was just a block away from Big Ed's house. Then I saw a pistol flash as my backside window was shattered. Glass hit my face as I ducked. I didn't know if more shots were going to be fired. Beer bottles were thrown as they hit my top and hood. I reached for a stick under my seat. Then I heard two more shots as Crow and Big Ed came running out of the house. This time it was Big Ed shooting. I turned toward the side street and hit the gas. I could see VSL vatos running. I wanted to run all of them over. Big Ed ran all the way down the street shooting.

Boom! Boom! Boom! It pierced my ears. I noticed porch lights coming on and people looking out of their windows. I yelled to Big Ed. "Give me the cuete! The pigs are going to come. They'll search your pad!"

Big Ed ran up quickly and handed me the gun. It was a small .380 semi-automatic. I hit the gas to a side street. I knew the cops were going to be coming. They knew if shots were fired on that street, it had to be Big Ed. The only place I could think of was Angelina's house, a jaina I had been seeing. If I could only make it to her house I would be ok.

A few blocks away I pulled into her driveway on the side of her house. I grabbed the cuete and quickly ran to knock on her door. As I knocked I kept looking down the street nervously. Her mother answered the door. She looked at me with disgust as she called her daughter. She had never liked me. I just wanted her to hurry up, and finally, she walked over to the door. She stepped out and hugged me.

"Hi, Loco. I missed you," said Angelina very calm.

"I missed you too," I said. "But check it out, I need a favor."

"What? Is something wrong?" she asked now worried.

I pulled out the gun and handed it to her.

"You need to hide this," I said.

"Huh, what's going on Loco? I don't know where to put this," she said confused.

"Please, just do it. The cops are looking for me. If your down for me then you'll hide it, NOW!" I said now more nervous than ever.

She didn't know what to think. She put the gun by her side and quickly walked in. I stood outside just knowing the cops were going to find me here. Angelina walked back out after a few minutes.

"Ok now, tell me what happened?" she asked.

"Did you hide it well?" I asked.

"Yes, don't you trust me?" she answered looking annoyed.

"I'm sorry. Don't even trip, I didn't kill anybody. Somebody just shot my window out, see," I said pointing toward my car. Angelina was a firme girl. Most of the time she was the only one that would actually listen to me. She had long dark brown hair with loose curls. She had brown eyes, with the longest eyelashes I had ever seen. She had always reminded me of an Aztec princess because of her perfect light brown skin. I met her while out cruising one night with Vince. She was cruising in a carload of jainas. Vince pulled up next to them and yelled for them to pull over. As we all stepped out of the car, Vince pulled out a joint for them. The jainas were all giggling and flirting except Angelina. She just sat in the car, very quietly. She caught my eye when she glanced over to her homegirls. We locked eyes and I thought I had seen an angel. I looked at her homegirls with tattoos on them, hair combed out, with globs of lipstick and makeup. They were smoking weed and talking about fighting. Vince was enjoying himself. He liked the rough girls. I walked over to her and began talking to her. It was as if we had known each other all of our lives. She was out cruising only because her homegirls begged her to go. I couldn't stop looking into her eyes. I knew that someday I would end up with her. I could feel it. But not right now. My life was too crazy for her. The last thing I wanted to do was to drag her into the hell I was in.

She gave me a hug and I didn't want to let go.

"I get so worried about you, Joaquin."

I didn't know what to say. I loved my barrio and I would do whatever it took. I could never go back. It would never be the same for me because it was no longer about a street or neighborhood. It was about a carnal dying. It was about pain. It was about revenge.

As I pulled away from her, two patrol cars pulled up behind my ranfla.

"Stand back from her! Put your hands behind your head. Drop to your knees!" yelled the cop as he pulled out his gun. Angelina stood back not knowing what to do. The other officer slowly walked up and handcuffed me. Angelina's mother opened the door.

"Angelina! Come inside!" I heard her yell. She quickly walked up and kissed me. Then she ran into the house with her mother. I could hear her mother yelling from the inside of the house. The other officers were standing next to my car, and they noticed my window shattered. I was pushed up against the car and searched. I just stood there with a look of not caring.

"What the hell did I do this time?" I asked smartly.

"Shut up, you stupid Mexican!" said the small stocky cop that was searching me. I could feel the cuffs digging into my wrists.

"Where's it at, punk?" asked one of the officers.

"Where is what at? What the hell are you talking about? I've been here all night," I said. I knew I wasn't fooling them. But they still couldn't find the gun.

"You really think your tough huh, Mr. Loco, the leader of Apache! You just look like a punk to me," said the cop. He looked back at the other officers. He was trying to provoke me. I just stared at him with total hate. If looks could kill, he would have been dead, buried and forgotten.

"What boy? You trying to act tough with me? I'll slap you around like a girl. You don't scare me," said the cop.

I just held it all in. I knew that someday I would have my payback. What was the use in fighting? You never won against cops anyhow. Then a detective pulled up with an unmarked car. I recognized him. He used to be a cop when Vince was still alive. He slowly looked at my window, then inside my vehicle. Then he walked toward me.

"Did you find a gun?" said the detective.

"No, we couldn't find anything," said the cop next to me. "I think he dumped it on a side street."

I didn't even bother to say anything. The detective knocked on Angelina's door to ask them questions. Nobody answered as the lights went off.

"What happened tonight?" asked the detective as he stood in front of me.

"I already told this officer that I was here all night. My window has been broken for a while now," I answered.

"Oh, so you just leave the shattered glass on your back seat?" said the detective as he walked me to his car.

"Your under arrest for a gang shooting," he said as he pushed me into his back seat. I didn't even fight or argue about it. I knew that they had nothing on me. And if some of those people testified against me, I would just shoot their house up, or have one of the homies do it. I didn't care. I knew it was just a matter of time before I got locked up. I was transported to the police station. The back seat was smaller than any back seat I had ever seen. I could still feel the cuffs cutting into my skin even more. Here I was, arrested for a shooting I didn't even do. Oh well, I thought. Big Ed would have taken the rap for me.

The detective pulled into the station driveway and stopped. The whole station had a large fence around it. Everybody had to go through a security gate. It was two stories high with big tinted windows. There was a small box with a numerical pad next to the gate. The detective punched a code in and the gate opened. As he drove in I felt the feeling of drowning. I knew my mother and father would be worried. He drove toward the back of the building to a garage door. The large door slowly lifted up as we drove inside. I turned to see the door come down behind us.

The detective stepped out and opened the back door. I stepped out and looked around. It was a cold garage made of solid brick and concrete. The bricks were painted white with names carved into them. I quickly read some of my homies names. We were buzzed in through a big metal door. My cuffs were taken off and he walked me inside. We walked down a brightly lit hallway to a small cell. I stepped into the cell and heard the large heavy door slam and lock. It was cold and I noticed the walls were also painted white. It had a sink and a toilet with no toilet paper. I laughed to myself thinking 'I'm glad I don't gotta go.' There was a concrete bench next to the door with gang carvings. I laid down and closed my eyes. I rubbed my wrists because it felt as if the cuffs were still on me. Before I knew it I fell asleep.

"Joaquín, come out," said an officer. I quickly woke up confused. I had forgotten where I was at. I stood up and walked out.

"Follow me," he said as we walked down a long hallway. I was taken into a small room and fingerprinted. Prints were taken of each finger and thumb. The officer didn't say a word to me the entire time. He had an annoyed look on his face. After the prints were done the officer handed me a tissue so I could wipe the excess ink from my hands. Then I had to stand as he took a picture of me.

The detective that arrested me walked in.

"Did you see if he had any tattoos?" he asked the officer.

"No, I didn't get to that yet" he answered.

"Oh ok. Well, you can go, I'll take it from here," he said.

Then the officer finished filling out a paper and walked out.

He had me empty my pockets and checked my shoes, I guess to make sure I wasn't concealing anything.

"So do you have any tattoo's?" he asked.

"Yeah," I answered as I lifted my shirt. He wrote it down on a form and asked, " Is that all you have?"

"Yeah, that's all I need," I answered.

He looked at me as if for the first time.

"My name is Detective Robert. I've been following your gang for some time now. I know about your best friend Vince."

I looked away from him. What the hell did he mean, following my gang around? He had the nerve to bring Vince up.

"Can I ask you something?" asked the detective. He motioned me to sit down on a small bench.

"Yeah, I guess," I answered as I took the seat.

"Why do you do this? What fun is there in hurting others all of the time? You're still young. If you keep this up, you'll end up in prison. Your not a juvenile anymore. And believe me, it's no fun in prison."

"What do you care. I do what I do. Just like you do what you do. That's just life," I answered. I looked at this detective.

I wondered what his angle was. Why the hell did he care if I went to prison or not?

"It doesn't have to be that way. You don't have to be involved in gangs. Why do you want to hurt others just because they're from the other side of town?"

I couldn't believe this idiot. How could he sit there and tell me about gangbanging? If he knew Vince was my best friend, then he should understand my hate towards VSL. Just like when a cop gets killed, no matter what, cops are going to carry hate toward the killer. They won't rest until the killer is rotting behind bars. But I can't put Vince's killers behind bars. I don't own a jail. So my justice for Vince's death is through fights, stabbing, and murder.

"Am I under arrest or what? If not then let me go," I said looking at the detective up and down.

The detective looked at me and shook his head. He didn't understand me. And I didn't understand him. What did I care about this pig? He never did anything for me.

"Yes, you are under arrest," he said.

"For what? What the hell did I do!" I yelled.

"We're linking you to shooting within city limits and possession of a firearm. You're lucky you didn't hit anybody," he said.

"You're crazy. You know that I didn't have any gun. I'll be out as soon as I go to court," I said.

I couldn't believe it. Taking me to jail with no proof. I didn't care anyway. They would have to release me in court. The detective read me my rights and put me back into the cell. I wished there was a way to call home. I knew that the cops were going to search my house. They wanted to find the gun badly. I hoped my mother and father wouldn't worry about me too much. I hated breaking their hearts all of the time. My father had such high expectations for me, and now I was just another cholo acting crazy.

Two hours later and I heard an officer unlocking the door.

"Time to go to county jail," said the officer. " Turn around so I can cuff you," said the voice of a woman.

I was cuffed and walked back down the hallway. A door was opened leading back into the garage. The female officer carried a plastic bag with my property, all the things in my pockets, money, papers and a small cross. I was put into the small cramped back seat again. The large door and gate were opened and closed once again as the vehicle moved forward. I was being transported to the county jail, which was located in the next city some twenty minutes away.

6

The drive to county jail was the longest twenty minutes of my life. It was night time. I looked around from the back seat of the patrol car as we drove on the freeway. I could see people in passing cars trying to look in to see who was arrested. I remembered always doing that myself. It seemed funny that now I was in this car, cuffed. The officer had the radio on a country station, playing at a low volume. I wondered if detectives in suits had already searched my house. I could already imagine my mothers face when the detectives knocked. She'd probably freak out, thinking I had been shot or was dead.

As we pulled into the driveway to the jail, I felt a sick feeling in my stomach. Would they find out about the vato I shot? I didn't want to live the rest of my life in jail or prison. As we drove closer to the jail I could see two large gates we had to go through. The first gate made of fencing and barbed wire opened as we pulled in towards it. Then the second solid metal gate also opened. As we drove into a huge parking garage I could see other patrol cars. I looked back toward the metal gate. It was slowly closing behind us. The officer parked the patrol car and stepped out to open the back door for me. I stepped out and stretched my legs. We walked toward a small metal door, and she pushed a small button and a buzzer was heard.

We walked into a small lobby with other prisoners. They were all looking down, some drunk, some ashamed. I sat down and was asked my name and address. The cuffs were taken off. I noticed other vatos in there, but nobody seemed to pay any attention to me. I was told to sit and wait. It was a large room with rows of chairs. Everyone here was waiting to be put into a cell. A big screen t.v. was against one wall, some prisoners watching it. They watched a show with no interest, with empty eyes. Then I noticed payphones against the wall. I had to call my mother.

I dialed my house number and waited. The rings seemed to take forever. Then I heard the receiver being picked up.

My mother's voice said "Hello."

"Hello, mama, it's me Joaquín," I said.

"Mijo, ¿dónde estás? I've been so worried," she said. I could hear her voice cracking as if she had been crying all day long.

"It's ok, I've been arrested. But don't worry because I didn't do it." It was breaking my heart to hear my mother this way. I knew that I wasn't the son she had expected me to be. I was always in trouble, always in fights. Once she found a gun under my mattress. When she questioned me about it, I ignored her. Some nights I would come home with blood on my shirts and my fists bleeding from punching. She would stay up some nights until I came home.

"The detectives came over mijo. They tore your room apart,

telling us that you're a bad person. They even questioned your brother. Are you going to stay there now?" she asked.

"No, they can't keep me here. I didn't do it, and I'm sure I'll get out when I go to court. They have to take me to court within a few days. Don't worry about me, mama. I'll be ok," I answered trying to comfort her.

"Ok, mijo, I'll be praying for you," she said as she hung up.

I slowly put the phone back on the receiver. Then I sat down to watch the t.v. until my name was called.

"Joaquín!" yelled the officer.

"I'm here," I said as I walked toward the desk. There were five sheriffs booking inmates in and typing information into computers. I was asked information about everything, my date of birth, my social security number, and anything else they thought they should know. Then I was asked to go into a small room to change clothes. Inside the room, I was given orange pants a white t-shirt and orange pullover. An officer stood there and watched as I handed him my clothes. I laughed to myself wondering if this pig liked looking at naked men all day long. I changed into the clothes that were given to me and walked out of the room. I sat on a long bench and waited for others to also change.

"Follow me," said a sheriff to the six of us waiting, that by now had changed. I stood up and we followed him through three long hallways. All I could hear was our footsteps echoing and the sheriff's handcuffs clanking against his belt. We were taken into a large two-story room with cells built all around. It was late, so I was handed a small dinner bag that had two sandwiches, an orange, and a styrofoam cup. Then the sheriff handed me a blanket rolled up with a small plastic bag inside. I was told to go upstairs to room thirty-four. It was quiet as I walked up the steps. I could feel others watching me from their cells. I wondered if I knew any of them.

The cells were built with two bunk beds, a sink with a mirror, toilet, chair, and small table. It had enough room to do pushups and sit-ups. The cell door closed behind me, and I heard the lock click. I had always thought that jail had iron bars for each cell. This cell had a solid metal door with a long rectangular window in the center. I was the only person in this two-man cell. I threw the blanket down on the bottom bed as I sat down on the chair facing the table, opening my dinner bag. I hadn't eaten in several hours, so I quickly ate the sandwich as I gulped down cups of water from the sink. Then I slowly peeled the orange and savored each slice, thinking about the oranges my mother would buy. After the orange was gone I walked to the sink and washed up.

I reached for the blanket and unrolled it. Inside was a towel and a pillowcase. Then I opened the plastic bag with paper, envelopes, toothbrush, toothpaste, pencil, and comb. I brushed my teeth and laid down. It was a long day, a day I wanted to forget. Now Angelina's mother would never like me. I was arrested right in front of their house. I hope her mother doesn't tow my car, I thought.

I was awakened by a door unlocking. There were loud noises as each cell unlocked. I could hear all of the inmates walking down. I quickly got up and looked out of my cell door window. My door was open as I heard that breakfast was being served. It was already morning. I quickly washed my face and stepped out of my cell. I followed everyone half asleep to a cafeteria full of inmates. It was segregated with Whites, Blacks, and Mexicans all sitting in their distinct groups. I waited in line to get my tray of food. They were serving cereal, orange juice, and an apple. I overlooked all of the tables trying to see where I was going to sit. All of the

Raza was sitting on the far end, I didn't recognize anyone. As I held my tray I walked towards them, wide awake. I noticed all the seats were taken. I didn't know what to do as they all turned to look at me. They were all older with big mustaches and goatees. The craziest looking vato stood up, "Hey ese, you can sit here. I'm already done."

"Orale ese, gracias," I answered as he stood up and dumped his tray. I sat down and nodded to the other vatos.

"Soy Joaquín de Barrio Apache," I said as I looked at everyone, not knowing what was going to happen. They all looked at me, as the biggest vato said, "¿Qué onda? I'm Cyclone. There are no Barrios here, ese, nomÿs Raza."

"Orale," I answered. I wondered what he meant by that. Everything I stood for was for Apache, my barrio. They all began shaking my hand as a sheriff walked by.

"Hurry up! It's not that much and it ain't that good! Eat and go back to your cells!" he yelled as he walked past us. All of the vatos began eating and getting up to dump their trays. I didn't say another word as I walked back up to my cell. It was six in the morning as I laid back to fall asleep.

I woke up a few hours later still locked in the cell. I stood up and washed my face in the small sink. I looked in the mirror. I couldn't believe I was in here, locked up like an animal. I paced back and forth, occasionally looking out of the small cell window. I tried to sit down and write a letter to Angelina, but after half a page I couldn't think of anything else to write. I heard my lock click open again and I heard gente talking. I opened my door and looked downstairs. Everyone was in line to go to lunch. I folded the letter and put it under the mattress. I walked down the steps and got in line. I waited my turn for my tray of sandwiches and fruit. This time I found a chair where all of the Raza was at. I sat down and nodded to all of the vatos. They all nodded back and ate lunch. The sheriffs gave us about 10 minutes to get a tray, eat lunch and go back to our cells. After lunch there I was again, with nothing to do but lay down. I carved Barrio Apache into the desk with the pencil they gave me.

We were let out of our cells a few hours later. Vatos walked to the showers, phones and t.v.'s. I took a stroll to the indoor handball court. It felt good to breathe fresh air. The court was indoor with a large canvas for the roof. Because the roof wasn't solid it would let fresh air come in. Some of the homeboys were playing handball.

"What's up homie, what's your name again?" asked a veterano playing handball.

"Joaquín, but the homeboys call me Loco," I answered.

"My name is Smiley," he said as he held his hand out.

I shook his hand and noticed Emiliano Zapata tattooed on his forearm.

"That's a firme tat, ese," I said.

"Gracias. I've had it for years now," he answered. Smiley was short and stocky, with "Brown Pride" tattooed on top of his right eyebrow. His head was shaved and a thick mustache connected to his goatee. He seemed calm yet always cautious. He pulled out a bag of tobacco and papers and rolled a cigarette.

"You want one?" he asked.

"Chale, no thanks. I don't smoke," I answered.

"Good, it's a bad habit," he said as he licked the paper and rolled it. On the wall was a lighter for the inmates. He walked over and lit his cigarette as I stood watching the vatos play handball. He walked back and sat down.

"So what are you here for? When do you get out?" I asked.

"I've been here so long, I don't even know why I'm in here

anymore. I had a court date so they transported me here for a couple of days.

"I've been in the pinta since I was about your age," he said.

I looked at him and guessed he was in his thirties.

"Orale, so when do you get out?" I asked.

"I still got about six more years. So what did you do?" he asked.

"Well, they say that I did a shooting. But these pigs don't got nada on me," I answered. "So... what barrio are you from?" I asked.

"Does that matter!" he answered. He put his cigarette out and stood up to face me. I stood straight and looked into his eyes.

"What, ese? I just asked a simple question," I said not really knowing what was going on.

"Can't you see! Are you blind o qué vato? All that barrio trash is for nada! In here our Raza sticks together," he said as he forced himself to quiet down.

"What are you saying? My camarada died for my barrio. It's all I got," I said feeling confused and angry at the same time. Smiley looked as if he was going to start throwing punches. I was ready to fight too. A la brava, to the death. I would never let a man put me down, even with the chance of losing. His eyes turned harder, more murderous.

"You got a lot of heart, ese, standing up to me," he said holding out his hand.

"I'm down for mine," I said as we shook hands Chicano style. "Simón your down, homie, but ask yourself this. Are you down to fight for the right reasons? I can tell that you're a leader. I knew from the second you got here. But let me tell you something vato, you're aiming your anger in the wrong direction," said Smiley.

I looked down letting his words sink in. He reminded me of the things my father would tell me. I understood everything Smiley was trying to tell me. But Vince died for my barrio, so I had to back it up forever. How the hell was this vato going to know how it was on the calles now? I would never show any type of compassion or mercy to VSL.

"My best friend was killed by another barrio. I will never forget or forgive that. I swore that I would kill every single one of them punks from VSL. Even if I do life in la pinta for it," I answered. I meant every word coming out of my mouth. "Look homie, your gonna learn. Believe me, sooner or later your gonna learn," he said as we were called back to our cells. I could feel myself getting pissed as I walked up the steps. My Raza getting along is a nice dream, but it would never happen.

I sat in the chair inside my cell. I felt the rage build up in me as I thought about what Smiley had said. How could any of these vatos ever expect me to get along with VSL? I hated everything about them punks. These veteranos in here didn't know what I felt. They'd been in these cells for too long. There was no way for me to let my anger out sitting in this suffocating cell. So I laid down and did push-ups until I couldn't lift myself up anymore until my arms felt as if they were burning.

Two days passed and I had two more days until my court date. It was the same thing every single day. Woke up at six for breakfast, then at twelve for lunch. Then we would be let out of our cells into the small indoor yard until it was dinner time at six. I played dominoes with some of the vatos when we were let out for a few hours. Smiley kept at my side telling me stories about la pinta. His court date was on the same day as mine. During our time in the small yard, we would go to the handball court, taking turns doing different combinations of exercises, from a jumping jack to squat, to a push-up and standing back up again. He said that the homeboys would do these exercises every day in the pinta. But not every pinta had the same combination of exercises.

I wondered if Angelina knew I was still in jail. There was no way to call her. I didn't want to call collect and get her in trouble. Being away from her actually made me miss her, even though I ignored her most of the time when I was out. I made up my mind to visit her first as soon as I was released. I walked to a payphone and called my primo Alfredo collect.

"Hey, it's me, Joaquin," I said as soon as he accepted my call.

"ORALE!" he said sounding excited. "How are you doing primo? I heard about what happened."

"Oh yeah? Who did you hear it from?" I asked.

"I went to your pad and your Jefito told me. He looked like he was pissed vato," he said.

"I haven't even talked to him. I don't know what to say," I said. "I should be out when I go to court. These pigs don't have nothing on me."

"Cool, ese, that's good to hear. You don't belong there. Is there anything you want me to tell anybody?" he asked.

I thought about it for a second.

"Simón. I want you to tell Angelina that I'll be out in a couple of days. And tell the homeboys to stay up, y que rifa Barrio Apache," I said.

"Damn right, homeboy, we're forever putting them chavalas de VSL down. Ok homie, stay trucha," Alfredo said as he hung up the phone.

It felt good to talk to someone back in the barrio. I hoped it was only a matter of days until I got out of here. First thing I wanted to do was iron some Dickies and take a cold shower. Wearing an orange carrot suit wasn't my idea of dressing firme. This jail time was nada. I knew that I could handle a long stretch. All the stories about fights and getting punked and bullied didn't happen to me. Everything in here was about respect and intimidation. As long as I stood my ground I knew I would be ok. I got a bed, food and a gang of homeboys to kick it with. But if it was my choice I'd rather be on the calles, kicking back with the homeboys or relaxing with Angelina. Smiley told me to not get my hopes up when I got to court. Sometimes the judge gave other court dates. So you just go back to jail and wait it out. Unless you have feria to bail out.

"Joaquín! You got a visit. Go to door five," yelled the sheriff as my door unlocked. I wondered who it was. Maybe it was Big Ed and Crow, or maybe even Angelina. I quickly washed my face and dried off. I wet my hair and combed it back. I didn't want to look tore up in case it was her. I walked down a small hallway to the visitors center. I reached door five and opened it. My mother and father were both sitting there staring at me. The small room had a stool with glass between the inmates and visitors. You had to talk over a phone because the glass was soundproof. I didn't expect them to visit me. I didn't want them to see me like this. I saw the tears in my mother's eyes. I lifted the phone at the same time she did.

"Mijo, are you ok?" she asked as tears came down her face.

"Mama, don't cry. I'm ok. Please, you know that I don't like to see you like this," I answered.

She pulled out a tissue from her purse and wiped her tears. Sitting in front of my mother was the hardest thing for me. I couldn't stand the fact that my mother was crying. I couldn't stand the fact that I was in front of her, with glass between us.

"My friends tell me that you're not going to get out. That you did something very bad," she said now looking right at me.

"I didn't do nada. I go to court tomorrow and I'm pretty positive that they'll let me out. So don't worry, it's at one thirty in the courthouse. You can go if you want," I said trying to make her feel better.

The entire time my father was sitting there patiently. Holding my mother's hand and looking down. He took the phone from her.

"Hello, mijo."

"Hi, I'm sorry that this happened," I said before giving him a chance to talk.

"Look, son, we can't take any more of this. I can't take any more of this," he said.

I couldn't look at my father straight in his face. I could feel his eyes burning into me.

"Whenever you get out of here," he said as he looked around then back at me, "I want you to get all of your clothes and leave."

I felt my heart sink.

"Why? You're just going to put me out into the street, just like that? I'm your son!" I yelled.

"Where's my son? I don't see the boy I taught right or wrong. I don't see the boy that loved our people. I don't see the boy I brought up to show respect and give honor. All I see is another cholo, another trouble maker. Do you think I don't know what you and your friends do? I didn't work all of my life so you could be a gangster. I didn't raise you so I could have my house shot at some day. I never thought I'd ever say this to you son, but you shame me. My own blood sitting in jail, Like a bum!" he said holding back tears.

He hung the phone up and looked back up at me. I felt as if I was stabbed in the heart. I could see the pain in his eyes as he stood up and opened the door to the booth. My mother whispered I love you and followed behind my father. I just sat there, not really knowing how to feel. I felt angry although I knew that I couldn't be angry. I brought all of this on myself. I never imagined the day my own father would turn his back to me. How could he? Especially when I needed him the most. What was I going to do, and where was I going to go? I felt that pain in my chest, the pain you feel when you're alone, or like when somebody dies, knowing that there is nothing you can do. You can't take that pain away no matter what you do. It was the same pain I felt when Vince was lowered into the ground.

I walked out of the visitation room and walked towards my cell. How could my father do that to me? I had never done anything to him. I had always shown respect and love for him and my mother. Why couldn't he understand what was going on in the calles? I didn't want this kind of vida. I ignored everyone as I slowly walked in as the door shut behind me. I couldn't take this anymore. The only man that I ever respected no longer wanted me in his house. I had never felt this alone in my entire life. What would my childhood heroes have done? There was no revolution, no war, no nothing. Just fights, guns and barrios. How could he say that he was ashamed of me, and say I was a bum? Those were the worst words he had ever said to me.

In my cell, the hours dragged and I couldn't stop thinking about my father's words.

"What's wrong, homie," asked Smiley during dinner.

"Everything ese, I feel like walls are closing in on me," I

answered.

"It can't be that bad, bro. Everything in this life happens for a reason. We all have a destiny," said Smiley.

We stopped talking because the sheriff was walking by. I continued to eat my food until he walked away.

"Can I tell you something?" I asked.

"Simón, of course, ese," said Smiley.

"I hate all of this gangbanging, bro. But no matter what I can't see an end to it. Do you really think I like to watch my back all day long? I never asked for this lifestyle! I feel like I was forced into it. It feels like I'm on a rollercoaster that won't stop. It goes faster and faster as each day passes," I said.

Smiley looked at me. I could see that he wanted to tell me a lot of things. But in the situation we were in, he couldn't. He ate some of his dinner then said, "You just do what you feel is right. Don't ever do something just because everyone expects you to. I've been here for years, and for what? I thought I was doing the right thing, backing up my barrio. But where are my homeboys now? I'll tell you where they're at. They're at home with their kids and ladies. Do they ever come to visit me, or at least write me a wila? Chale, out of sight, out of mind."

I totally understood Smiley. He really made me think about my situation. But I was too far gone; I was already lost. I just had too much hate for VSL. It was either leave the barrio and the gang or ride all the way to the end. There is no room for half-stepping in this vida loca. To me, vatos that don't ride all the way are showing a sign of weakness. And I could never let myself be weak. I sat and listened to everything Smiley said. He was a veterano that earned my respect. He was the kind of vato that I wanted to be someday. That is if I ever made it to be his age.

I woke up the next day with energy. I knew that I was going to court. After lunch, the sheriff began calling out names. Everyone called out stood in line for court. I was one of the last vatos called. I was the only Mexican going to court back in my town. We all stood still as the sheriff cuffed our hands and shackled our feet. Then we walked in a single file line outside to the hallway, then into a small van with bars on the windows. It felt good to be driving down the freeway. It had only been five days, but a lot had changed in those five days. I now had no place to live. Even if I was released, I had nowhere to go. We drove into a small driveway leading to the back of the courthouse. We drove into a garage, parked, got out of the vehicle and were led

inside. I was put into a small cell to wait for my case to come up. After most of the inmates were called to court, it was finally my turn. The sheriff opened the cell and took off the handcuffs, leaving the shackles on.

The shackles clanked as I walked into the courtroom. I instantly saw my mother sitting in the back row. I nodded my head to her. My name was called and I hardly paid any attention to it. The judge and D.A. were talking back and forth about me in legal terms I had never heard before. I was asked if I had an attorney, and I answered no. A public defender was appointed to me.

"Have you ever been in trouble before, Joaquín?" asked the judge.

"No," I answered

"So, you've never been arrested?" said the judge.

"No, I haven't. This is my first time in jail," I answered.

He nodded and looked back at the police file. As he was reading I could feel my blood pulsing through my brain, thinking of a million things at once. The judge looked at the district attorney, "What exactly is he being held for?"

"Well, he was stopped for a shooting. The police believed he was involved. He was later found a few blocks away with his backside window shattered," said the D.A.

"Yes, I can read that he was arrested for a shooting. But I can't understand the grounds for arresting him. No gun was found, he wasn't at the scene of the crime. And there have been no witnesses saying that he was the shooter. Was anybody shot?" asked the judge.

"No your honor, but our detectives are still investigating his involvement," said the D.A.

"Ok, well I recommend Joaquín be released on O.R. He is to be released today and will be given another court date," said the judge. "Do you have anything more to say," asked the judge as he looked back toward the D.A.

"No your honor. We can have him back to court in thirty days. That will be sufficient time for the detectives to work," said the D.A.

I didn't understand most of what they were saying, but I knew what released today meant. I felt a great relief come over me. I looked at my mother as she smiled at me. I was given court papers and taken back to the small cell.

"Congratulations," said the sheriff sarcastically.

"Yeah, thanks. So when do I get released?" I asked not wanting to argue.

"Well, you got to go back to the jail for now. They'll call you after dinner to roll your blanket and sheets up. They'll tell you what to do.

"Thanks," I answered feeling relieved. I felt each second tick as I waited to be taken back to the county jail.

Once I was back in my cell, I tried to sleep until dinner

time. I tossed and turned with each minute. During dinner, I said my goodbyes to the homeboys. Smiley was happy that I was going to be released.

"Don't ever forget what I've told you, ese," said Smiley.

"Chale, I'll never forget homie," I said as I gave him an abrazo. I knew that he was going to go back to la pinta. I wondered if I would ever see that vato again.

7

———

I let the cool night air fill my lungs as I walked out of the county jail. I had called Big Ed to pick me up. My clothes were wrinkled and I tried to straighten my creases out. Where the hell was I going to go? I had no place to live. I wondered if my father would let me stay the night. It was midnight. I waited nearly thirty minutes before I saw Big Ed driving down the road towards the jail. From a car full of homeboys I could hear loud music playing. As the car came closer, I could see that it was Chuey and Crow with him.

"¡Qué onda!" yelled the homeboys as they all jumped out of the car, hugging me and shaking my hand.

I couldn't help but smile. It felt good to be with my carnales.

"Let's go to a taco truck so I can eat some real food," I said laughing.

"Simón bro, it's on me," said Big Ed sitting in the driver's seat. I sat passenger as we drove to the freeway.

At the taco truck, I ordered un burrito de carnitas y cuatro tacos de asada. And to drown it all down, a fruit punch Jarrito drink. Simón, I thought to myself. This is where I belong, eating Mexican food in my barrio, with my homies around me.

After the taco truck, I asked them to drop me off at my parents chante. Big Ed drove off, so I walked to the porch, but I hesitated to knock. I stood there quietly for roughly five minutes before I had the courage to knock. I could hear my mothers voice inside as the porch light turned on. The door opened and it was my mother.

"Mijo, come here!" she said as she hugged me. "Are you hungry? Are you tired?" she asked.

"I'm ok, I just need a shower," I answered.

Then I saw my father walking toward the door. I thought he was going to slam the door in my face. Instead, he hugged me and said, "I love you, mijo."

"I love you too, dad," I said. "I want to know if I can stay tonight. I'll find a place to live tomorrow."

"Si, that's ok. I never said that I hated you. Go ahead and wash up and rest on your bed. I just wish that things could be different."

"Gracias dad... I really appreciate it," I said as I walked toward my room.

My room was a mess from the cops searching it. I tried to clean and pick up, but I was too exhausted. Instead, I took a good shower, laid down and slept on my own bed. Tomorrow was going to be a busy day. I needed to get all of my clothes and things together. Plus I wanted to see Angelina.

The next day I woke up to the smell of my mother's food. Simón, I never realized how good that smell was until I ate in jail. I could hear the grease popping as my mother cooked bacon and eggs. I could hear my carnalito watching television and talking to my mother. I knew that I had to leave this house, but I felt happy that I was out of jail. I took my time to iron my light grey Dickies and a white t-shirt. I figured that this might be my last morning here. After getting dressed I slowly walked toward the kitchen. I sat down at the kitchen table.

"Good morning, mom," I said.

"Si, it is a good morning. My son's out of that terrible cage," she said as she kissed me on my forehead. I think the love of a mother is the deepest of love. I know that no matter what, my mother will always be there for me. My father was at work so I ate breakfast with my little brother and mother.

"I'll be back. I need to get my car," I said as I walked out of the door. Angelina had kept my car in her driveway so the cops wouldn't impound it. She lived a few blocks away so I decided to walk. I passed by the small liquor store and walked through the park. There were graffiti markings on just about every wall in the barrio. The streets seemed to shine from all the fragments of broken glass shattered by winos and drunks throughout the years. It was still early so none of the homeboys were around. It felt firme to just take a stroll with no drama. Even though this barrio was torn up, it was the place I loved.

When I reached her house I could see my ranfla. I reached the door and knocked, hoping she was home. The door opened and there she stood. She smiled and said "Joaquín!" and hugged me.

"I got out last night. How are you doing?" I asked.

"I've been so worried about you. My mother keeps getting on my case because of your car. I didn't know what to do," said Angelina.

It felt good to see her again. It's not like I didn't like her. I actually liked her so much that I didn't want her pulled into my troubles. I could never let her know how I really felt about her. My vida was too complicated. She looked beautiful as I stood back and looked at her. Her eyes had a softness about them that I had never seen in a jaina before.

"I need to talk to you, Joaquín," said Angelina.

"Sure, did you want to leave o que?"

"Let's go to the park," she answered.

"Orale, get in," I said as I pulled out my car keys from my pocket.

"Is your mom going to trip if you leave with me?" I asked.

"No, she isn't here," she answered.

I put my key in the ignition and started the ranfla. As I backed out of her driveway, Angelina sat close to me. I turned on the cassette deck to oldies playing. I drove into the large cement court at the park. I still didn't see any homeboys kicking back. I stepped out from my ranfla and walked over to her side to open the door for her. We sat under the nearest tree with the most shade.

"So, what's up?" I asked.

"A lot of things Joaquín. First of all, my mom hates you. I don't know what to do because I really care about you. She wants me to stop seeing you. She says that your nothing but trouble. And that you have nothing to offer me."

I sat there, listening to what she was saying.

"Well, maybe she's right," I said.

"What! Why do you say that?" she asked irritated.

"Look, Angelina, you know how my life is. Damn, I just got out of jail. You don't want anybody like me," I said.

"Why do you say that? You don't know what I want. Why

are you pushing yourself away from me? I thought you liked being with me?" she said.

"Your mother's right. What the hell do I have to offer you? Nothing. My dad kicked me out of the house. VSL wants me dead. I got another court date where I might do more time. I can't offer you nothing," I said.

Angelina looked down toward the grass. I could see tears coming down her face, tears that landed on her lap.

"What's wrong? Don't cry," I said as I put my arm around her. She turned toward me and hugged me.

"I don't know how to tell you. I don't want you to be mad," she said through her tears.

"Tell me what? It's ok whatever it is. I won't get mad," I answered wondering what she wanted to say.

She stopped hugging me and sat back up, wiping her tears. She looked at me and said, "I'm pregnant. I just found out two days ago."

I couldn't believe it. "Are you sure?" I asked.

"Yes, the doctor said that I'm three months.... Are you mad at me Joaquín?" she asked.

"Of course not. Why would I be mad?" I answered. I truly felt happy, but how was I going to take care of her. I had no money, no house, no nothing.

"Really! You're not mad?" she asked.

"No," I answered.

She smiled, kissed me and said: "I love you Joaquín."

I didn't know what to say. I just hugged her without saying a word. Why was my life so messed up? What kind of father was I going to be? Would I even live long enough to see my kid grow up?

"Have you told your parents?" I asked.

"No way! They'll kick me out for sure. That's why I don't

know what to do," she answered.

"Don't worry, mija, I'll figure out a way to take care of you and our baby," I said not having any idea of what I was going to do.

We talked a little while longer then I dropped her off at her house. She kissed me goodbye. "Call me later," she said.

"Ok, I will. But I'm going to be out of town for a few days. I need to figure out what I'm going to do," I said.

"Oh wait, you forgot something," she said as she ran into her house. Then she ran back out with a wrapped towel and handed me Big Ed's cuete.

"Oh I forgot about that," I said.

"I don't really want you to have it. But if my parents find it they'll be mad. Just be careful," said Angelina as she walked into her house.

I drove back toward my chante and packed. My trunk was full of clothes, Lowrider magazines, and pictures.

"Where are you going, mijo?" asked my mother.

"I don't know yet, but don't worry. I'll be fine." Then I kissed her on her cheek and got in my car. My mother stood outside watching me as I drove off. I didn't want to talk to anyone, not even the homeboys. I just needed to get out of town. I didn't have gas or money so I forced myself to ask Big Ed for a loan. He was outside sitting on his porch when I pulled up.

"Hey homie, what's going on?" asked Big Ed as I sat next to him on the porch.

"I need to get away vato. My dad kicked me out and I got all my stuff in the trunk," I answered.

"Damn.... just like that?" said, Big Ed.

"Yeah, my dad told me when I was locked up."

"I wish I could help you out. My mom will trip if I let any more homies stay here," said Big Ed.

"Chale. I would never ask you to house me, bro. But check it out. I was wondering if you could loan me a little feria? I'll pay you back as soon as I can," I said.

I wasn't sure how Big Ed was going to react. As soon as I asked he reached into his pocket. He pulled out a thick wad of bills and handed me two hundred.

"Here man, don't even trip on paying me back. I know you wouldn't ask me unless you really needed it," said Big Ed as he put the rest back into his pocket. I didn't know what to say or how to thank him.

"Are you sure?" I asked still holding the money.

"Damn right I'm sure. How long have I known you? You're like my brother. Naw ese, you are my brother. Oh yeah, I don't know what you did with that cuete. Do you still have it?" asked Big Ed.

"Simón, I just got it back a little while ago," I answered.

"Well, just go ahead and hold on to it," he said.

"Gracias, carnal. I owe you one," I said as I put the bills into my pocket. Then I shook his hand with a firm grip, puro Chicano style, man to man. I gave him a big abrazo as I got up to leave. Now I had enough feria to fill my tank up, eat and get a motel room. I knew that as long as I had homeboys like this, I would always have someone to turn too, even if I had nowhere to go.

8

As I was driving on the freeway heading out of town, I had no idea where to go. It was a crazy feeling just driving and not knowing where to. The sun was hot as the heat beat down on my ranfla. I didn't have air conditioning so all of my windows were down. Besides, I didn't have a back side window. Most of the freeway was empty. Nobody wanted to drive in this temperature. Then an idea came to me. I had a tio that lived about a hundred miles away. I hadn't seen him since I was a kid. He was what my father called 'the black sheep of the family.' He had done five years in prison when he was younger. I never knew what he did wrong. But I knew I had his address written on a card he had sent to my familia for Christmas. My father would hardly ever talk about his younger brother. But regardless of what my father thought of him, I was on my way to visit him. I now sat up straight and pushed the gas down a little harder. With a destination to reach it made the heat tolerable. I didn't even know if he would recognize me. I figured since I had the address, I would just have to find the Mexican side of town. All I had to do was just follow the taco stands, bars and Mexican grocery stores with pinatas hanging from the windows.

As I reached the town where my tio lived, I pulled over to a gas station to fill up. I asked the Mexican attendant where the barrio was. He pointed toward the left and said, "The barrio is that way."

"Orale. I'm looking for a street named Club House way. Do you know where it is?" I asked.

The attendant rubbed his chin in deep thought. "No se, I don't recognize that street," he answered.

"Are you sure? I have a letter that was sent from this town, "I said.

"Pues, maybe I don't remember it," he answered.

"Ok, pues gracias," I said as I started my car and drove off. I figured that I would just cruise the barrio until I ran into the street I was looking for. I drove for roughly forty-five minutes and found nothing. I saw a park with some cholos playing handball. I pulled over to ask them, hoping they could help me.

"Hey homies, can I ask you vatos a question?" I asked.

"Sure, what's up?" answered the oldest looking vato. He was about my age but skinny and pale. He walked over to my car.

"I'm looking for this street, have you heard of it? It's called Club House Way."

"There's no street in this barrio with that name, ese. Who are you looking for anyway?" he asked.

"I'm looking for my ti6. I'm from out of town," I answered.

"Who's your ti6, maybe I know him. Everyone in this town knows each other."

"His name is Roberto Ponsillo," I said.

"Are you talking about Cuerno?" he asked.

"I don't know his nickname... all I know is his real name," I said.

The cholo quickly called his homies over to where we were, then asked them, "What is Cuerno's real name?"

The youngest cholo said, "Isn't it Roberto... Roberto Ponsillo."

"What! How do you know my uncle's name?" I asked. I could tell that they were holding something back. Now I was confused. They knew what his name was, but they didn't know where Club House Way was.

"Everybody knows Cuerno in this town. He doesn't live in the barrio, though. He lives in the new houses," said the skinny cholo.

"And where are the new houses?" I asked.

"Back that way," he said as he pointed in the direction opposite from the barrio."

"So your really Cuerno's nephew?" he asked.

"Simón, why? What's the big deal about it," I asked not understanding. This was getting stranger as it went along.

"I just didn't know that he had familia, that's all," he answered.

"So I just head that way?" I asked as I sat back into my car.

"Simón," he said.

As I drove toward the newer part of town, the houses got larger and larger. Finally, I found Club House Way, and I slowly drove looking at all the addresses. Towards the end of the street was a small court, and I saw that the house I was looking for stood there, two stories high with huge pillars on each side of the front door. I double checked the address on the card my tio had sent. Sure enough, it was the same. In the driveway was a brand new black convertible Mercedes.

The yard was flawless with red and purple flowers bordering the house. I closed my car door and walked towards the front door of the house. I didn't know what to expect. I looked back toward my car one more time, and I felt like driving away. I had never been in a neighborhood like this, much less knocking on the door of a house this big. I bit down on my tongue and pushed the doorbell. I could hear Mexican music playing inside and a voice coming closer and closer to the door. I held my breath as it opened.

"Who the hell are you?" asked a tall stocky man with no shirt. His voice was deep and powerful. He had Brown Pride tattooed across his upper chest. His hair was short, slicked back and he had a thick mustache.

"It's me tió..." I said hoping he remembered me.

He stared at me then it suddenly hit him. "Joaquin!" he said as he hugged me. I hugged him back, truly happy to see him.

I heard a woman's voice, "Who is it Cuerno?"

"Come here! It's my nephew Joaquín," he yelled back.

"Come in, mijo, come in. I want you to meet my wife Isabel. She is your tia," he said as he stepped back and let me walk into his house. The second I stepped into the house, I couldn't help but notice the beauty. It had black carpet with bright white walls and huge portraits of Aztec imagery on fancy frames. One portrait had pyramids with warriors killing a Spaniard. The other was of the Aztec calendar. There were black leather couches in the middle of a huge living room as big as my parent's entire house. On one end of the room was a big fifty-one-inch t.v. screen, surround sound and home stereo. On the opposite wall was an aquarium that practically went from wall to wall. I could tell that the tank was salt water by the bright colored scales on the fish. As I sat down on the couch I saw a beautiful elegant woman walk in. She looked like a superstar, a model. I couldn't help but notice her beauty.

"Hola," she said as I stood up to shake her hand. She was smiling as she sat next to my tio.

"Hello," I said totally amazed by everything, my tio, his house, and my aunt.

"So how have you been mijo? How's your dad?" asked my tió.

"Well, I've been ok. My dad's just been working," I answered.

"Good... Good. Are you hungry?" he asked.

"Um, well..." I said as I felt my stomach ache from hunger.

"Isabel, can you heat something up?" he said as he turned to his wife.

"Of course," she said as she quickly stood up and walked toward the kitchen.

"No familia of mine is going to be hungry in my house," he said.

"Gracias, tió, it's been a long day for me," I answered.

"DAMN! It feels good to see you. I'm so happy that you came by."

"Yeah, I'm happy to see you también. This is a firme house tió. I wish I could live in a place like this someday," I said admiring the furniture.

"Well, why not? You can anything in this world mijo. All you got to do is be hungry enough to go for it," he said laughing. "How long has it been now mijo, the last time I saw you... you were just a chavalio," he said.

"I know, it's been awhile. I came by cause I needed somewhere to go," I said.

"Hey! Are you in trouble?" he asked now looking concerned.

"Oh no, nothing like that. I just had some problems at home," I said.

My tió looked towards the floor thinking. Then he said, "Well if you don't want to tell me it's ok. Believe me, I know what it's like to have problems at home. Esta es tu casa for as long as you want. And I won't take no for an answer," he said now looking me in the eye. I could see that my tió was a man to be taken seriously and with respect.

"Thank you tió, I really appreciate that," I said.

"De nada. Come on, let's eat," he said as he stood up from the couch and walked toward the kitchen.

I followed him into a dining room where there was a huge oak table and chairs. I could smell the warm Mexican food. I couldn't believe my tió was living this good all this time. I wondered why my father wouldn't communicate with him if he was so successful. As we sat and talked I found out that my tió was the owner of a Mexican music record company, a detail shop and two Mexican restaurants. He seemed nice as he told me stories of my father and him when they were kids.

After eating he helped me get my clothes out of the trunk. Then I followed him upstairs to a guest room with its own shower and bathroom. The room even had a twenty-seven-inch t.v., VCR, and CD player. He said that it was my room for as long as I wanted. I folded my clothes and put them into a dresser in the corner of the room. I looked out of my window, and I could see the view of the neighborhood. There were brand new cars on every single driveway, so my ranfla looked out of place. I hid my gun under the dresser, making sure it was pushed all the way back toward the wall.

I opened the closet and saw an ironing board and iron. I began to crease my Ben Davis and shirt, and then I took a good cold shower. I hadn't felt this relaxed in a long time.

There was something about my tió that was powerful. He reminded me so much of how I wanted to be when I was younger. I knew that I was only a hundred miles away from home. But as far as I was concerned, it felt like I was across the world. Here there was no drama about the barrio, no detectives knowing my name, no nada. I knew I had to figure out what to do about Angelina, and it felt as if I could think more clearly here.

I finished my shower so I walked downstairs. I could hear my tió arguing with someone on the phone. It sounded like he was threatening someone. As soon as I reached the bottom of the stairs he quieted down.

I acted as if I hadn't heard anything. He hung up and asked, "Hey, how are you feeling now?"

"Good, really good," I said.

"Do you want to go for a ride with me? I got to go talk to someone," he said as he grabbed the keys from the coffee table.

"Sure, just let me go grab my sunglasses," I said as I hurried back up the stairs. I got my locs and thought about it for a second, then grabbed my cuete from under the dresser. I checked to make sure it was loaded. When he was threatening the person on the phone he had said that he was going right over. I didn't know what was happening, but in my barrio, you always stayed packed.

I came down the stairs, my cuete hidden and he said, "Let's go." We walked out of his house. We both got into his black Mercedes and drove off.

"Where are we going?" I asked trying not to act nervous, although I was.

"O, necesito hablar con este hombre. I figured you could come along and keep me company," he said. As we drove, it seemed as if he waved at everyone in town. We drove straight through the town for miles until we finally reached a small dirt road where there was a two-story house with dogs tied up by the side garage. My uncle looked toward me and said, "I'll be right back, ok? This will only take a minute." He left the car running so the air condition would keep the car cool. I nodded as he stepped out and walked towards the house. This situation didn't feel right. I noticed all of the shades down in the house. Were we at the person's house that my tió was threatening? Maybe I was just nervous because of everything that was going on with me, back home. I always felt as if someone was out to get me. I had a gut feeling about this place because I never trusted anyone. I noticed two brand new Lincoln Town Cars on the side of the house, one had Sinaloa Mexico license plates on it. I pushed the button for my window to roll down and turned the car off. Then I could hear yelling and arguing. I thought, what the hell have I gotten myself into?' I slowly stepped out and cocked my gun to make sure my tió was ok. Suddenly, I saw a man thrown out of the front window, glass shattering everywhere. His shirt was ripped off and his face was bloody. He was trying to stand up but was too dazed to keep his balance. I just stood there trying to understand what was going on. I heard furniture crashing as my tió came running outside toward the man laying on the ground. I ran closer as the dogs barked violently.

"If you don't pay me, I'll kill your whole familia!" yelled my tió as he went to the man on the ground and picked him up by his neck. The blood on the man's face was dripping as he tried to fight my uncle off. My uncle punched him then pulled out a chrome forty-five and cocked it. It was as if he forgot I was there because he was in such a rage. I could see demons in his eyes as he pushed his gun into the man's mouth, making the man cut his lip with his own teeth. Just as this was happening a man ran out behind my tió with an AR-15 assault rifle. I didn't hesitate or think twice as I raised up my gun and aimed. Two shots and the man fell. With this my uncle looked up and saw me, still aiming at the man. He turned and began pistol-whipping the man I had just shot. I could hear the man yelping. The man that was thrown out of the window was still laying on the ground. My tió reached into both of the men's pockets and pulled out two rolls of money. Then he spits at both of them and yelled, "Tienes dos dias!"

He ran towards the car and we both jumped in. He was sweating and I noticed his shirt was ripped.

"Where did you get that pistola!" he asked as he drove toward his house.

"I had it from back home," I answered. He stayed quiet for a few seconds. I didn't know if he was upset with me or not.

"Where did you learn to have such fast reflections?" he asked.

"From my barrio," I said.

He began laughing. "You are truly a blessing mijo! You saved my life!" he said as he pulled me close to him and hugged me. I was still in shock, not knowing what was going on.

"Your ok, mijo. Eres un hombre que vives a la brava!" he said.

"With us together, nothing can stop us. We're FAMILIA!"

I couldn't help but smile seeing my tió so happy.

As soon as we got home my tió took my gun. He hid it in case the cops would show up, even though he was pretty confident that nothing like that was going to happen. I was totally confused. In my town, I would have been in jail already or at least in hiding. I walked upstairs to take a shower and change clothes. I didn't want any gun powder on me. I sat on the bed in my new room as my tió walked in. He had taken a shower and had also changed his clothes.

"Look, what you did today took a lot of guts. Don't worry about the cops here... those guys won't call them. They shouldn't even be in this country, so if they call the cops they'll get deported. Now, I got some questions," said my tió.

"I did it for you, tió. But I'll answer anything you want to know," I said.

"Ok, well here's the first question. Why are you really here? Don't get me wrong. I like you being here."

"My dad kicked me out of the house. I just got out of jail for a shooting. I had nowhere else to go. And I just found out that my girlfriend's pregnant." Saying this felt strange because I had never called Angelina my girlfriend. "Look tió, I don't have no money, no nothing to offer her."

He just nodded his head. "Well as far as your father kicking you out, I hope you understand why he did it. Your father is a good man. I'm sure that's why he kept you from me. And as far as going to jail, I got the best lawyers in this part of the state. Don't you worry about that."

I just sat there listening to my ti6. Here was a man that I should have had growing up because he was like me. I loved my father and always respected him. But the last few years had been crazy. My father didn't understand the hate and rage I had toward VSL. He didn't understand about avenging my homeboy Vince's death.

"So do you really like this girlfriend of yours?" he asked.

"Simón, she's beautiful tió. She makes me want to live a better vida, but I can't no matter how hard I try," I said.

"Look. You saved my life today. I would have been dead. Out of any day, you showed up on a day I really needed you, and

I will never forget that. Second, there is more you need to know. I wasn't sure if I could tell you when you first arrived. But now I know que eres hombre de las calles. As far as your girlfriend, don't worry about her. I'll show you how to make money. I'll help you and your girlfriend as much as I can," said my tió as he reached into his pocket. "I think this belongs to you," handing me the roll of money he took from the man I had shot. I quickly glanced at it as I put it in my pocket; I would count it later.

I guess I had a look of concern because my tió began laughing as he put his hand on my shoulder. "What are you worried about!" he said.

"Nada," I said.

"Well, rest up. And tomorrow I will show you how I do business," he said as he walked out of the room. I didn't know what to think. I felt like my head was spinning. I had just shot a man, and there was no police, no waiting for retaliation, no mob of homeboys all excited ready to go to war. I remembered the wad of money in my pocket. So I quickly pulled it out and unrolled it. A rubber band was holding it all together. I couldn't believe my eyes as I counted two thousand dollars in twenties and fifties. I had never seen this much money in my life, and here I acquired it in a matter of two gunshots. I looked towards the t.v. and noticed a phone. I needed to call Angelina to let her know that I was alright. I dialed her number and waited for her answer.

"Hello," I said, "is Angelina there?"

Her mother didn't answer me. I could hear her tell Angelina that it was for her.

"Hello," said Angelina sounding out of breath from running to the phone.

"Hi, it's me Joaquín," I said.

"Oooh Joaquín, are you ok? I was hoping you would call me."

"Yeah girl, I'm doing firme. I'm visiting my tió. I think he has some work for me," I said.

"Really, that's good," she said sounding relieved.

"Hey, have you told your parents anything?" I asked.

"No way! I already told you what would happen," she said whispering.

"Well don't even trip girl, porque I already got some feria. I'll be down in a few days to see you," I said.

"Ok, I'll be here."

"I don't want to stay long... it's my tió's phone," I said as we said our good-bye's and hung up.

For the rest of the night, I just relaxed and watched television. It had been a long time since I had just relaxed. I had a lot of worries, but they felt so far away. I think I was going to like it here, and I knew I would learn a lot from my tió. This was the kind of life I wanted, a big house, nice car and Angelina by my side.

9

The next day I woke up to the smell of papas with eggs and freshly warmed tortillas. For a second I thought I was back home. Then I realized I was at my tió's house. I got up and ironed and took a shower. I wondered how my tió would show me to make money. Was he going to get me a job at his restaurant, or record company? It would be firme to be able to get a chante and take care of Angelina. As I was getting dressed I heard a knock at the door.

"Mijo, come downstairs for some breakfast," said my tió.

"I'll be right there," I said as I put on my socks and shoes. I walked downstairs and saw two men sitting with my tió around the dining room table. They all looked at me and said, "Buenos dias." I nodded my head to them. I sat down to eat as I heard them talking about packages they had just brought from Mexico. I heard them say that they had been driving all night. I saw my tió hand them a bag full of something, and I heard him say it was money. I didn't want them to think I was listening to their business so I kept eating. They shook hands and left. I finished my breakfast just as my tia sat down to eat. She almost cooks as good as my mother, I thought.

"Are you done?" asked my tió.

"Yeah, it was good," I said looking toward Isabel.

"Thank you," she answered smiling.

"Orale pues, vamos al negocio. I got a lot to show you," said my tió as he kissed Isabel on the forehead.

"Be careful, Cuerno," she said as we walked out.

I stood up and put my plate in the sink, then I followed him to the garage. Inside he had boxes of CD's and cassettes, posters of famous Mexican groups hung up all around the walls, signed to Cuerno.

"This is one of my businesses. I record and release all of these groups," he said as he pulled out several CD's from a box to show me. I looked at the CD covers. Most were of Mexicano's holding pistols and assault rifles. I had never seen groups like these.

Even the titles were crazy, "El poder de la mafia," "La vida no vale nada," "Traficantes." All of the titles had something to do with drugs, mafia, and crime.

"So is this music like Mariachi music?" I asked. I had never known Mexican music to be any different. The only time I would hear Mexican music was at weddings and quinceaneras.

"No... haven't you heard of groups like Los Originates de San Juan, Los 4 Grandes del Norte or Los Tigres del Norte? They all sing about shootouts with Judiciales, el trafico de drogas y la vida in Mexico," said my tió.

"I never knew about this kind of music. I always thought it was all love songs," I said.

"Hehe... No, this is the kind of music you should learn to

appreciate. Corridos, instead of all this rap music you probably listen to," he said.

"Here, bring these CD's with us," he said as I followed him out of the garage. He pushed a button on his garage opener and the garage door closed.

I opened the first CD and slid it into his deck. My tió turned his stereo up loud as the intro of the song played. It was of a traficante crossing the border in Tijuana as the border patrol asked him questions. The whole car shook as the bass guitar played with the accordion filling up the midrange and tweeters. I had never taken the time to hear this type of Mexican music, so for the first time, I listened to the words. It was about a traficante hiding drugs in the car and smuggling it across the border. Then the next song was about a fugitive that the FBI wanted. In the song, the fugitive was in a shoot out with U.S. agents and got away to Mexico to become a legend. I thought this music was really firme. It was totally hard-core, like gangster rap.

We drove toward the foothills as my tió began talking to me. "Look, before I tell you how to make feria, you need to promise me something," he said looking towards me and driving.

"Sure, anything ti6," I said.

"You have to promise me that you will only make enough money to start your own business. I don't want you to end up like me, sitting in the pinta for years," he said.

"Ok, I promise. So, tell me," I said.

"I smuggle marijuana and crank here from Mexico. I've been doing it for years, and that's why your father didn't bring you around me. I started just like you, broke with nowhere to go. It was either starve and die, or do what I had to do. But you can't do it forever. Don't follow my footsteps. I don't care if you open a donut shop or flower shop, as long as you make your money legit. I will show you everything so you can take care of your lady. I own four different casas in the foothills miles apart from each other, so we are going to one of them now. They are all in someone else's name, not mine. I never keep anything in my home, not even plastic baggies. Remember that, never ever keep anything in your home. What I do is have a family live at each house and live a normal life. They both have real jobs, drivers license and kids that go to school. They live rent-free, I pay for electricity and all other bills. I use these houses to store scales, pistols, and drugs. I never let anybody see these houses... your the first," he explained.

My tió was a very smart man. Why hadn't I ever thought of doing this before? Instead, all I did was fight against other vatos all day. Everything seemed like a perfect plan.

"So do you have any questions?" asked my tió.

"Yeah, in what amounts do you sell? I've never slanged drugs in my life. I don't even know how to weigh it," I said.

My tió laughed and said, "I sell in any amount. And don't worry about weighing it because I'll show you how. It's not that hard. I get mota for twenty-five dollars each pound, straight from the mountains of Michoacan. By the time it gets transported here, it costs about a hundred and fifty dollars a pound. I need to pay the driver and bribe the Mexican judiciales. It's not worth it unless I bring a few hundred at a time. Once it's here I can sell each one for three hundred and fifty dollars. So that means that every two hundred pounds I can profit forty thousand dollars. And I do that every other week," he said smiling.

"Damn, are you serious? That's a lot of money," I said.

"Oh, haha. That's just pocket change, mijo. Let me tell you

where the real money is at. Do they have crank in your barrio?" he asked.

"Simón, but I think most older vatos do it, and White fools. But my good homeboy Big Ed sells bud in town to everyone," I answered.

"Well, I get crank manufactured in the outskirts of Tijuana. I get it in it's purest form. If vatos here would do it, they would have a heart attack," he said laughing.

"I know what you're talking about. Some of my homeboys do it at parties. It's like chunks of rock and powder and smells like something rotten," I said.

"Yeah, it's all made from chemicals. It sells better than coke because it's cheaper and the high last eight times longer. When I get it, I cut it with ephedrine. It's a chemical used for chicken feed and medicines. Out of one pound, I can make two pounds, each one selling for three thousand dollars. So if I bring in forty pounds of pure crank, I can make eighty pounds. And this is every week or so. I can never have enough. Some vatos try to make three or four pounds out of one, but this never works. All you get is complaints because it's not strong enough anymore. Do you think I care about the idiot's out there doing it? Let them ruin their lives. They would get it whether it's from me or somebody else. In this life I've learned one thing; we are nobody without money. And the more money we have, the more important we become. When your father and I were young, we worked in the fields for very little, sometimes less than minimum wage. I would see the farm owners driving around with brand new trucks, bought with our sweat. You could never imagine the sweat and dust I wiped from my brow year after year. And when the checks came in once a week, I didn't even have enough money to buy myself a decent home. How do you think that made me feel? I'm a man, damn it! But no matter how hard I worked, no matter how many hours of overtime I put in, I could never make anything of myself. In the United States of America, you are either rich and respected or your just a nobody," he said with his voice deeper than ever. I could see the veins in his neck pulsating as he became angry thinking of the past. I sat there not saying anything, I didn't want to make him angrier. He calmed down as we reached our destination.

It was a small modest house with a garage on the side. Children were playing in the yard as we walked up to the door and knocked. A man opened the door and handed my tió keys to the garage. I followed my tió as he walked to a door on the backside of the building. We walked in as I closed the door behind us. I couldn't believe what I saw, stacks and stacks of marijuana, all bagged up in pounds. The walls had insulation to keep the cool air inside. We walked to a table where two triple beam scales were.

"Let me show you how to use this," he said pointing to one of the scales.

"I've seen my homeboy use one of those before," I said.

"Well a pound weights four hundred and forty-eight grams, a half pound weighs two hundred and twenty-four grams, and so on and so on," he said as he showed me how to slide the weights to the right amount. I soon learned how to weigh pounds, half pounds, quarter pounds and ounces. Anything less than an ounce wasn't worth weighing, according to my tió. Then he showed me how to break down a pound of crank, this time with more precision than the weed. He recommended wearing gloves when breaking it up because it would go into your skin pores. I had to be careful to make sure it didn't crumble because nobody wanted to buy dust.

It was better sold as a solid rock. Crank came in different colors, but normally it was a creme peanut butter shade. The color depended on how long the chemicals were cooked and how many cuts were put into it. After a few hours of weighing, bagging to transport crank and weed, we walked back out. My tió locked the door behind us and walked over to the man sitting on his porch. They shook hands and we got into the car and left.

"So your homeboy sells marijuana?" asked my tió.

"Simón, but he doesn't sell in big amounts. He buys it from some White guy from out of town. I think the most Big Ed buys is half a pound every two or three days," I said.

"Good, if he buys it from a White guy, then most likely he's paying a high price. Call your homeboy up and tell him that you got a connection for weed. Tell him to tell his White boy connect that he can get him pounds cheaper than anybody else. Then tell me what he says. I know I can match any price in this valley," he said.

I nodded in agreement. Big Ed was going to trip when I told him all of this. I already had two thousand dollars and I hadn't even started yet.

Once we got back to the house I went up to my room. I picked up the phone and called Big Ed.

"Hey vato, it's me, ese," I said.

"¿Qué onda homie? Where have you been?" he asked.

"I had to get away from everything for a while. So how's the barrio doing, ese?" I asked.

"It's been quiet bro, at least for now," he answered.

"Well check it out, do you got your pager with you?" I asked.

"Simón, why?" he said.

"I need to talk to you about something, but from a pay phone. I'll page you with a number right now, I'm going down the street to a market or something," I said.

"Yeah, go ahead. I'll be waiting, bro," he answered.

"Orale, I'll talk to you in a minute," I said as I hung the phone up. I walked downstairs and told my tió I was just going to the store. He waved as I closed the front door behind me. I drove to the nearest gas station and got change. I parked next to the phone and paged Big Ed with the payphone number. I didn't have to wait long.

"So what's going on, ese?" said Big Ed on the phone.

"I need to ask you something bro, about your weed sales," I said.

"Well, what do you need to know?" he answered.

"I need to know how much you pay for your bud. I'm with my tió from out of town and I know I can get a good price," I said.

"Oh really! Well how much can you get the libra's for?" he asked.

"I'm not sure yet. But my tió said that he can beat your connects price. Matter of fact he said it's so cheap that you can supply your connect," I said feeling confident.

"Damn, well I buy my pounds for five hundred, but it's fresh and green. There is cheaper bud out there but it's all dirt weed," he said.

"No man, this bud looks good. I don't smoke it but I know how it looks and it's good. The pounds are kept in a cool place, and they are all huge buds with no shake. They're compressed but since they are fresh you can fluff them out," I said repeating everything my tió had taught me earlier.

"Can he supply in big amounts? My connect sells to a lot of vatos all over. I think he buys like twenty pounds once a week," he said.

"Can you find out how much he pays for it?" I asked.

"Simón, let me call him right now. Give me fifteen minutes and I'll call you back to this number," said Big Ed as I hung the phone up.

I quickly got in my car and headed back toward the house. My tió was sitting on a lawn chair on his front yard. I got out of my ranfla and sat next to him.

"Tió, I just talked to my homeboy. He wanted to know how much you have the pounds for. He said that his connect buys 'em twenty at a time," I said.

"Twenty at a time… let me think… Ok, I'll tell you what to tell him. I'll give them to you for two hundred and fifty, that way I can make a hundred profit from each one. I recommend that you add another hundred to each one. If you want to give your homeboy part of your profit or if he wants to raise it more is up to him. That will make you a two thousand dollar profit. How often does he buy?" he asked.

"He said that he buys twenty once a week," I said.

"Well, there you have it. You can make two grand a week. That's eight thousand a month," said my tió.

"Orale, that sounds firme. I'm going to go back to the phone," I said walking back to my car.

I had just arrived at the phone when I could hear it ring. I quickly stepped out and answered it.

"Hello."

"It's me, bro, I just talked to the vato," said Big Ed sounding excited.

"Well, what did he say?" I asked.

"He pays four hundred for each pound. He didn't believe me that I could get it cheaper. He wants to see what it looks like. How much do you sell them for?" he asked.

"I can give them to you for three hundred and fifty dollars each. It's up to you if you want to raise it. But if he buys twenty from me at a time I'll give you five hundred dollars each time we set up the drop. All you have to do is have him meet me wherever, like a motel room or a house or something. I don't want to go to his house, because it might be hot with cops," I said sounding like my tió.

"Orale, well he said that he's ready to buy some tomorrow. Can you bring some and see if he likes it? Show him one of the pounds and if it's like you say, he'll pay for twenty up front right there," said Big Ed.

"Yeah, I'll do that. I'll be in Apache around noon time... I'll page you and put four twenty as a code and the number of where I'm at," I said.

"Cool bro, I'll see you tomorrow. Stay trucha, ese," said Big Ed.

This was all too good to be true. By tomorrow I was going to make another two thousand dollars, and that is before paying Big Ed his five hundred. I drove back to the house and set the deal up with my tió. In the morning he would bring the twenty pounds to a friends house, and there I would hide it in my vehicle. I would drive during the lunch hour so the freeway wouldn't be alone and deserted. My tió said to never transport during the night hours, where a Mexican driving is more of a target to the cops.

I walked up to my room and took a good shower. It'd been a long day. Then I counted my money, putting all the hundreds, fifties and twenties together. As I laid down to sleep I thought of Angelina. Soon I would buy us a house and a brand new car. I would be able to help my parents and my little carnalito. My tió had said to think of a legitimate business to start, but I had no idea what I wanted. This was going to be a brand new start for me. It felt as if I actually had a chance in this vida. My tió was right, with money you were somebody. That's why barrio's like Apache and VSL were treated with no respect because we lived in the poor sides of town and we never had money. Cops felt like they could do whatever they wanted, knowing that we couldn't fight them back. I didn't know anyone that could afford a lawyer. No one was forcing me to sell drugs. I thought about what options I had, and selling drugs looked like the only one.

10

___

After putting the clavo under my back seat I drove back to my barrio. A clavo was the hiding place where the weed was. I made sure I drove the speed limit, used my left and right signals when changing lanes and stopped at all stop signs. I exited the freeway and pulled into the Motel 6 parking lot. Once there I rented a room in the back of the building. I pulled into the parking space right in front of the room I rented and looked around. No one was watching. I quickly pulled my back seat up. I had two large carrying bags I had used for clothes. I put all of the pounds except one into the bags. Then I opened the door to my room and closed the door behind me. Once there I pulled the mattress to the side and laid each brick side by side on top of the box spring. Then I put the mattress back down and made sure the mattress lay level.

I picked up the phone and paged Big Ed. I remembered to put the four twenty code after the phone and room number.

I waited for a few minutes when the phone rang.

I answered it, "Hello."

"¿Qué onda, bro? Is everything all firme?" asked Big Ed.

"Yeah, I'm here in town. Where do you want to meet? I don't want anybody coming over here yet," I said.

"Just come over my pad. I'll have the vato meet us here," said Big Ed.

"Orale, I'll be right over," and I hung the phone up.

I put the two empty bags into the corner of the room and walked out, making sure I had the key. I felt less pressured knowing that I wasn't carrying twenty pounds anymore. After carrying that much weight, one pound felt like nothing. Big Ed was sitting on his porch waiting for me.

"Q-vo, ese," said Big Ed as we shook hands.

"What's up, homie," I said feeling good. It was strange. I hated my barrio but at the same time, I loved it. So much has happened but Barrio Apache was the only place I knew. There was no other place like my barrio.

"I called that vato, and he's coming right over in about thirty minutes," said Big Ed.

"Cool, that gives me enough time to fluff it out. It's all compressed right now," I said as I reached into my back seat and pulled it out. I put the pound into a paper bag and walked into Big Ed's chante.

"Let me check it out, bro," Big Ed told me eyeing the paper bag I was holding.

"Here," I said handing him the bag. He opened it and pulled out a big zip-lock plastic bag. The second he opened it I could smell the fresh bud.

"Damn, ese, this looks good!" he said smiling as he held the

"Thought it wasn't?" I asked as I sat down on the couch. I laid the pound on the coffee table. I began to break apart the large buds. Soon the buds were all fluffed out and covering the entire table. There was hardly any dry stems and leaves gathered under all of the buds.

"Well… what do you think?"

"Don't even trip, ese. I know he'll buy it," Big Ed replied.

A few minutes later a knock was heard. Big Ed walked over to the door and looked through the peephole. It was the weed connection.

"Hey, this is Black," Big Ed said to me as they both walked over to the couches.

"What's up. I'm Joaquín," I said standing up to shake his hand.

Black was tall, skinny with dirty blond hair. He had tattoo's of skulls, women, and demons holding swords and decapitated heads.

"Damn, this is the bud you got?" he said as he sat down and picked a bud up. He pulled out a small weed pipe and laid it on the table as he began to break one of the buds down. Once he pulled out the stems and seeds, he stuffed his pipe and lit up. I watched Big Ed and Black share the pipe, inhaling and exhaling large clouds of smoke. The smoke didn't bother me. I was only thinking of the money I was going to make.

"Hell yeah, man! This weed is good. How many did you bring?" he asked between his coughs. He picked up some of the buds feeling how fresh they were.

"How many do you want?" I asked.

"I'll take whatever you got, right now," He said pulling out a huge wad of hundred dollar bills.

"Orale, each pound is three hundred and seventy-five," said Big Ed. He added twenty-five dollars to each pound. He knew Black paid more than that price.

"Cool man, let's do this," said Black.

"I got twenty pounds right now, but I don't have em here. You'll have to follow me," I said.

"Cool man, however, you want to do it. So can you get this kind of bud consistently?" he asked.

"Hell yeah. I'll get you this bud every day if you want," I said feeling confident.

"Cool man, cool. I'll probably get twenty of these a week," he said counting out his money. "So... twenty pounds at three seventy is...?" he asked as he calculated in his head.

"It's seven thousand five hundred," I quickly answered.

"Ok," he said as he counted hundred after hundred.

"Don't you want to get the bud first?" I asked.

"Naw man, I trust you. I've been working with Big Ed for years now," he said laughing.

"Orale," I said as I looked at all of the hundreds on the table, laying on top of the bud. I recounted all of the money and then put the pound of bud back into a bag, handing it to Black.

"Just follow me," I said as we walked outside. Big Ed sat shotgun in my car and Black followed in his car. We drove toward the motel. I pulled out the money from my pocket and peeled out ten hundred dollar bills from the stack, "This is yours, carnal," I said.

"Hell yeah!" he said. "This is the quickest turn around I've ever done!" he said as he put the money in his pocket.

Once we reached the motel I handed my room key to Big Ed. He walked over to the room and had Black park right in front of it. I instructed Big Ed to put the bud in the bags. I was watching everything, making sure no cops came around. After a few minutes, Big Ed walked out of the room with the bags and handed them to Black. Black took them and put them in his trunk. He drove off as he waved.

"Damn ese! We got to do this more often," said Big Ed smiling.

"I know, bro, I know," and I drove back toward Big Ed's chante.

"Hey, do you want to make some real feria?" I asked.

"You know me, ese. I'm down for whatever," he said.

"Do you know anybody that buys CR?" I asked.

"Crank! Hell yeah, but I never had a good connect for it. Why? Don't tell me you got someone," he said excited.

"Simón, the same vato with the bud has a bunch of CR tambien," I said.

"Why didn't you leave town sooner?" said Big Ed laughing. I had never seen Big Ed so happy.

"Just find out how much crank he wants and I'll call you later before I leave town," I said.

"Orale," replied Big Ed.

We shook hands as I drove off toward Angelina's house. I now had made three thousand five hundred dollars. A few days ago I was broke with nothing to my name. I couldn't wait to tell Angelina about the money, but I wondered what she would say. Maybe she didn't need to know about how I made the money. After all, money is money. I put the volume up on my stereo, and Zap & Roger bumped more bounce to the ounce.

As soon as I pulled up next to Angelina's house, I knew something was wrong. I could see the window to her bedroom shattered on the driveway. I got off of the car and walked up to the door. Just as I was going to knock, Angelina's mother opened it.

"WHAT DO YOU WANT!" she yelled. "She isn't here! She is your problem now. I'm not having no damn grand kid from a cholo like you!" she screamed.

"What are you talking about?" I asked. " I just want to talk to Angelina," I said.

"I said she isn't here, and she will never be here. NOW LEAVE!" she demanded.

In shock, I walked back towards my car as her mother stared at me. I wondered what the hell was going on. I had just talked to her the night before. I needed to find her. She knew I was coming, so where would she be at? I drove around the barrio and didn't see anything. Then I remembered the park. She would know that I would look for her there. I quickly turned down the block that led me straight to the park.

As I drove into the large court, I could see her sitting on the bench by herself. She didn't look up to see me park. I slowly walked toward her. I could see that she was crying.

"Hey," I said as I stood next to her.

"Joaquín!" she said as she looked up at me and hugged me. She began crying uncontrollably.

"I don't know what to do... I... don't know where to go," she said between her sobs.

"What happened? I just came from your house. Your window was all shattered," I asked concerned.

"I got in a big fight this morning with my parents. I told them that you were going to come over. They started yelling at me and telling me that you were no good, that I was stupid for even talking to you. And that you cholo's belonged in prison forever. I got so angry that I told them I was pregnant from you," she explained as she continued to cry.

"Then my dad went to my room and starting yelling at me and throwing things. He shattered my window... I was so scared."

I listened to her as I looked around the park. "Well it's ok now, because I'm here now with you," I said.

———

She looked up toward me and stared right into my eyes, "Are you really there for me?" she asked.

"Yes, I really am here for you. Come on, lets go somewhere," I said as I stood up.

"But I don't even have clothes! I don't have nothing Joaquín," she said trying to stop her crying.

"Like I said, I'm here now. Don't worry about anything," I said.

She stood up and we walked toward my ranfla. I drove around town so she could calm down. I hated seeing her like this. I took her to a store to buy small necessities such as toothpaste, toothbrush and other things. Then we drove to some clothing stores and I bought her clothes and three pairs of shoes. It didn't cost much. I spent four hundred dollars on everything. I still had another two thousand one hundred dollars. After shopping, we drove to a motel room so she could clean up. I wondered what I would have done if I had never met my tió. What would she have done. I watched her brush her hair and do her makeup. She was a firme lady. I walked over and hugged her as she looked into the mirror. It was always her hugging me, but this time I felt like I needed to hold her. Things were going to change, for the both of us. She turned around as I kissed her on the lips. Simón, this was the lady I wanted to be with.

Once she finished doing her make-up again we drove around to look at apartments. I knew that I would have to go back to my tió's house, but I didn't want to bring her along. I didn't want her involved with what I was going to do. She would be better off in our hometown.

"So how did you get all of this money?" asked Angelina.

"I told you, my tió has a job for me," I answered.

"I'm not stupid Joaquín. I'l never tell you how to live your life, but I just worry about you," she said.

"Look, don't even worry. I'm going to work with my tió until our baby is born. Then I'll start a business... it's gonna be firme," I said holding her hand.

We looked at three apartments and none of the landlord's would accept us. Finally the last apartments we went to, the old landlord asked, "Can you afford this place? I charge three hundred and seventy five a month, and I want first and last months rent," he said.

"I'll tell you what sir, I can pay you for first and last months rent, plus two more months right now," I answered pulling out my wad of cash.

The old man looked at Angelina and then back at me. "You aren't going to have no loud parties are you?" he asked.

"No sir, nothing but peace and quiet," I said counting out the money.

"Ok young man. You got yourself a deal," he said as we shook hands. I counted out one thousand five hundred dollars.

"Here's your key, and I need you to fill these papers out. I'll get them from you tomorrow," he said as he handed me the forms to move in.

"Sure, thank you," I said smiling at Angelina. We walked over to the apartment and opened the door. It was a one bedroom with a large living room. It was perfect, light brown carpet and white ceiling and walls. Now we needed furniture; the place was empty. I could smell the shampoo from the carpet that had just been cleaned. Angelina hugged me, "Thank you," she said excited as she walked to the room and bathroom looking around. I slowly looked over the entire apartment. This was just going to be temporary. Soon I was going to have a house, like my tió's.

"Hey, I want you to stay in the motel room tonight. We need

to buy a bed tomorrow and turn the gas, electricity, phone and water on," I said.

"Aren't you going to stay with me tonight?" she asked.

"I can't. I gotta get back to my tió's. He's waiting for me, but I'll be back tomorrow, I said.

"Are you sure you'll be back?" she asked.

"Yes," I said as we walked out of the apartment and I locked it.

"So exactly how many months until your due?" I asked as we drove back to the motel room.

"I'm three months now. Just six more months and I'll pop," she said laughing.

"That's good. So I got six months to make as much money as possible," I said.

"You better be careful, Joaquín!" she said.

"Of course mija, of course," I said.

I drove to the motel room and dropped her off, promising that I would return tomorrow morning.

"Are you hungry?" I asked.

"No, not really," she answered.

I reached into my pocket and gave her a hundred dollar bill and kissed her. "This is in case you get hungry."

"Ok, thank you."

I pulled my head back to look at her face. She looked beautiful. I touched her cheek then drove off.

I drove straight to Big Ed's house to see about selling crank. Once I arrived there I asked to use his phone. I called the utilities and turned the phone on, as well as the water, gas and electricity. Since I didn't have bad credit, I didn't need a deposit.

"Orale, now that I got that out of the way, did you call that vato?" I asked.

"Ha, ha.... damn right I called, ese," He answered smiling.

"Well?" I asked.

"The vato buys two pounds at a time, and if you bring a sample tonight, he'll buy them tomorrow if he likes it," he said.

"Orale, that's all I need to know. So how much does he usually pay?" I asked.

"Well, if it's good like you say, he'll pay up to four hundred an ounce. That means that he'll pay six thousand four hundred dollars each pound," said Big Ed.

"Are you serious? How much does good crank go for an ounce?" I asked not believing that someone would pay six thousand four hundred for a pound. I remembered that my tió said he sells his pounds for three thousand dollars each.

"He'll turn around and sell that same ounce for six hundred. And he says that sometimes he buys up to four pounds a week. So I know that vato makes a gang of feria," said Big Ed.

"So, how much can you sell it for?" he asked.

"Hmm.... I can sell the pounds for five thousand each. That way you can make a thousand four hundred for each pound. Does that sound firme?" I asked.

"Hell yeah homie! It's on vato," he said smiling.

"Orale pues, I'm leaving. I'll call you when I got that sample," I said as I got back into my car and drove off.

As I drove back towards my tió's house I thought about my day. I had made one simple transaction and now had an apartment, gave Angelina a hundred dollars, and bought her clothes, and I still had five hundred dollars in my pocket. This was going to be firme. I could make a fortune, then I could help all of the homies out. Barrio Apache was going to be different. With this kind of money, VSL was going to bow down to Barrio Apache. Vince would have been proud of me.

I could see him now, slanging along with me.

As I pulled into my tió's driveway I could see that he had some friends over. I knocked as my ti6 opened the door.

"Hey mijo, you're back already?" he asked smiling.

I walked in and greeted his friends. Then I walked up to my room and pulled out all of the cash from my pockets. I counted all my ti6's money and put it under the mattress. Then I put the remaining money back into my pocket. I heard a knock, "Come in!" I said.

My tió walked in and asked, "Hey, how did everything go?"

I reached under the mattress and pulled out his money and handed it to him. He smiled and said, "See mijo, I knew you had it in you." He gave me a big abrazo.

"My camarada wants a sample of crank tonight. If his homie likes it, he'll buy two pounds tomorrow," I said.

"Hijole, your not playing around are you?" he said laughing deeply. "Yeah, I'll get you a sample after dinner. But right now come down with us. We're going to dinner. Isabel and I are going with my friends. I want you to meet them. They just came in from Sinaloa," he said.

"Ok, sounds good. I'm hungry, I haven't eaten all day," I said.

"Oh yeah, before I forget. Here's your pistola. You don't need to hide it anymore. Those guys at the house are dead. They tried going down to Mexico and they didn't even make it past Mexicali. Esos hombres, they had to learn the hard way... they don't call me Cuerno for nothing," he said handing me my gun.

"Gracias," I said as I put my pistol under the dresser again. I could see that my tió Cuerno could really be cold blooded if he had to be. I felt glad I was related to him.

I walked downstairs and we left to dinner. We ate at Red Lobster. I had never been in a restaurant like that before.

Hell, I had never even eaten at a Denny's. My tió laughed as I tried to crack open the snow crab legs. I had to crack it just right so the crab meat would slide right out. Then I could dip the meat into a small cup of melted butter. It was a trip seeing all of these white customers eating proper, dressed proper. Here I was, a cholo eating crab dipped in melted butter. I noticed people glancing at us, especially with my tió wearing three huge diamond rings, a Rolex watch and a leather jacket. My tfa was also nicely dressed all in black with large diamond earrings and a diamond necklace. I heard my tió make a remark about how poor this restaurant was, that all of the good restaurants were in San Francisco. During the entire time there we lived it up and joked around. It felt good to be here, Mexicano's living it up. My tió paid the entire bill and tipped the waitress forty dollars. I wished I'd brought Angelina.

After dinner, we went back home and my tió had someone drop off an eightball of crank for a sample. An eightball was an eighth of an ounce. I called Big Ed and made plans to meet him halfway. I didn't feel like driving another hundred miles back to Barrio Apache. We made plans to meet at a Wal-Mart store I had seen on the side of the freeway. By the time I left my tió's house, it was already night time. I played a cassette my tió gave me titled Los Traficantes. I still couldn't believe how much these corridos reminded me of gangster rap. Then I thought it would be tight to start a record company just like my tiós. But I didn't know a damn thing about Mexican music. I put the volume up as I drove to where the Wal-Mart was located. I exited the freeway and parked in the large lot. I walked in with the sample hidden in my shoe. As I walked in I saw Big Ed eating at the small Mcdonald's inside of the store. I glanced at him and walked into the restroom nearby. I checked to make sure it was empty as Big Ed followed me in.

"What's up, bro?" asked Big Ed.

"Just handling business. Here's the sample. Go ahead check it out," I said as I pulled the eightball out of my shoe. It was wrapped in plastic. Big Ed grabbed it from me and pulled the plastic apart. The smell of Crank traveled throughout the restroom in a matter of seconds. "Damn, now I know this is good," said Big Ed as he closed the plastic back around the Crank rock. "I'm pretty sure he'll like this, ese."

"Orale, just let me know as soon as you find out. Here's the number to my tió s pad," I said as I wrote the phone number on a piece of paper.

"I'll get at you as soon as I can," said Big Ed as we shook hands and walked out of the restroom. Big Ed walked out the parking lot as I shopped for some Dickies and t-shirts.

As I got home from Wal-Mart I was glad to see that my tió was home, his ranfla parked in the driveway. I wanted to ask him some questions about starting my own business. Before I had a chance to knock, my tía opened the door as she was leaving.

"Hi, Joaquin. I'm going to do some late night grocery shopping. Go ahead and go in. Cuerno's in the living room feeding the fish," said my tia Isabel.

"Ok, thank you," I said and walked in, closing the door behind me. I could hear my tió feeding the fish. I walked into the living room and sat on the couch.

"Hey, mijo! How did it go?" he asked as he sat on the couch facing me.

"Real good. He looked at it and said he could tell it was firme," I answered.

"Don't even worry, mijo. I don't get greedy like these other Mexicano's around here. I cut it, but I still leave it strong.

That way you're guaranteed that anyone that buys it will come back for more," said my tió.

"Well he said he'd call me tonight," I said.

"¿Pues, cómo esta todo en tu barrio?" he asked.

"It was kind of crazy when I got back into town. My lady got kicked out of her chante," I said.

"¿Qué? Are you serious?"

"Yeah, but she's ok now. With the feria I made I went ahead and got an apartment for her," I said.

"See what I mean, mijo? I told you I would show you how to make feria," said my tió smiling and sitting back comfortably on the couch.

"I really appreciate what you doing for me tió. I don't know where I would be if it wasn't for you," I said.

"Don't you ever worry about it. We are familia mijo, and nothing can ever get in the way of that," he said, now sitting straight looking proud.

I sat quiet for a second trying to think of what to say. I decided to tell him my idea of starting a record company. I was hoping he wouldn't think it was stupid.

"Well, I wanted to talk to you about something. I think I know what I want to do as far as a legit business," I said now looking determined.

"I want to start a record company like you. But instead of narcocorridos, I want to do Chicano gangster rap. I've never heard a Chicano tapper talk about the vida of gangs, barrios y drogas. And I think that I could sell a lot of CD's with that type of rap," I said.

My tió sat in deep thought, glancing at his aquarium. "That's a good idea, mijo. If that's what you want to do then I'll help you out. But I don't know a thing about rap music, mijo," he said.

"You don't have to know about rap music. I just want you to explain to me how the business works, how much it costs to record and make CD's. I have no idea. Once you have boxes of CD's in your house, how do you get them into the stores?" I asked.

"I can tell you everything. I know where the studios are at, where the manufacturing plant is. You need to find distributors to carry your CD's and put them in all of the record stores," said my tió. He explained everything to me, how to promote, record, distribute and sell CD's. We had been talking for over an hour when the phone rang.

"Hello... oh yeah, here's Joaquín," and my tió handed the phone over to me.

"Yeah," I said.

"It's me, Big Ed. The vato said it's all firme. Just come by tomorrow at one o'clock."

"Orale, I'll be there," I said hanging the phone up.

"It's all firme tió," I said. "I'll need two pounds of crank in the morning."

"You sure work fast mijo. I like that," he said.

After talking about the two pounds with my tió I walked upstairs to my room. It had been another long day. I called Angelina at the motel room to make sure she was ok. We talked for an hour, then I turned the lights off and fell asleep. Tomorrow would be another day to make money.

II

———————

The next morning was a good morning. I quickly ironed and took a shower. I wanted to be back in town to get Angelina before check out time. My tió had already hidden the two pounds of crank inside the back bumper of my car. There was a small opening for the package to snugly fit in. I thanked him then I drove off to meet Big Ed. Today I was going to make four thousand dollars, all in one simple transaction. I made sure I drove the speed limit all the way back into town. I could see the motel as I exited off the freeway. I felt happier than I had been in a long time. Before I would never think of my future, but now I actually had a future. With Angelina and the baby that was coming, I had to make a better life. As I pulled into the parking in front of the room I rented, Angelina looked out of the window. She quickly opened it and ran out to meet me.

"Hi baby," she said as she hugged me.

"Hi," I said as I held her in my arms. "You're already dressed?"

"Yes, I've been waiting for you," she replied.

"Orale, well let's get some breakfast. I haven't eaten. I wanted to eat with you," I said as she smiled and ran back into the room and brought out all of her bags. I opened my trunk to put the bags in.

"So where do you wanna eat?" I asked as Angelina sat in my passenger seat.

"I want to eat at the burrito place," she said smiling.

"Well, burritos it is mija," I said as I drove to the small Mexican stand located in Barrio Apache. Everyone from Apache grew up on that food. It was the best in town.

When we pulled up some of the homeboys were there. Dragon, Chuey, Tobo and Spider all walked up to my car as I stepped out.

"¿Qué onda vato? You've been hiding from us," joked Chuey as he gave me un abrazo. We all shook hands Chicano style. I had only been gone for a few days, but it seemed like an eternity since I had seen them. We were always together.

"So has VSL started any pleito?" I asked.

"Chale, them vatos know we'll put it down, ese," said Dragon.

"Check out my new tat, homie," said Spider as he pulled his shirt up. It read Apache across his chest, shaded in.

"That's tight, bro," I said looking at the detail.

"Hi guys," said Angelina as she stepped out of the car.

"Hi," they all said.

"Are you vatos hungry?" I asked.

"Well we were just trying to put our feria together to get some tacos," answered Chuey.

"Chale with that vato. Come in with us and get what you want," I said feeling good. "Breakfast today is on me."

"Are you sure homie?" said Dragon.

"Of course I'm sure," I said walking toward the front door of the stand.

"Besides, I want to talk to you about something," I said.

"Orale," said Chuey.

We all ordered our food and sat down putting two tables together. Angelina stood up and walked to the restroom.

"Things are going to be different for us," I said.

"What do you mean, ese?" asked Chuey.

"We are going to take this whole town over homie. I've been out of town and doing a lot of thinking. We have been wasting our time with these chavalas from VSL. It's time we make some feria... money controls everything," I said.

"What do you mean wasting our time with VSL? They killed your best friend, ese," said Dragon. I could tell I irritated him.

"No, ese. You're taking it all wrong. I hate them vatos, but we have been going at it all wrong. I'm still gonna smash on them punks every time I see them. But with money we have power. Money for lawyers when we get busted, money for guns when we need them and money to leave town if we have too," I explained.

"You're talking crazy now. I have no idea what you're talking about," said Tobo.

"Look vato, Angelina is going to come back any second. We'll talk about this later," I said. Then I pulled out my wad of money and handed each of them a hundred dollar bill. "This is what I'm talking about."

They all looked at each other in amazement.

"It's yours, a gift from me to my homeboys," I said.

They all shook my hand just as Angelina sat back down. We ate our food and I told them that we would hook up in a few hours. Again we shook hands as Angelina and I got back into my ranfla and drove off toward Big Ed's house.

"I need to stop at Big Ed's for a second," I said to Angelina.

"Ok," she replied.

"After we leave my homeboys, I want us to pick out some furniture for the apartment," I said.

She smiled, and I knew she was happy. Before reaching Big Ed's chante I remembered that I needed a pager. I drove to the small pager place a few blocks away from Big Ed's house. It only took a few minutes to buy, and then I immediately called my tió and gave him the number. I told him that I was on my way to a homies house.

As I reached Big Ed's house, I reversed into the driveway as he stepped out of his front door.

"Just in time, ese," said Big Ed as he walked down the front steps.

"So what's going on with that vato? Did you talk to him today?" I asked.

"Hell yeah, I talked to him. I already got the money on me," said Big Ed.

"Damn vato! He trusted you with that much feria?" I asked surprised.

"All I got is my word homie. These vatos know that I'm about business."

Then Big Ed reached into his pocket and pulled out a wad of hundreds. "Here's the ten G's for the pounds. I already took my part out."

I walked toward my bumper and looked around. Nobody was watching as I reached into the backside and pulled out the pounds. It was wrapped in plastic and duct tape. I handed it to Big Ed then shook his hand.

"I wanna talk to you about something later. Somehow I want the homeboys to make feria with us," I said.

"Orale, I was just thinking the same thing."

"Cool, well I'll be back later. I'm going shopping right now," I said.

Then I walked back toward the driver's side, sat down and said to Big Ed, "I'll see you in a while, carnal."

I drove off and as I drove on Morelos street, Angelina said concerned, "Joaquín, I don't want to get in your business or nothing, but promise me that you'll be careful," and she sat close to me. "I don't want to know about what you do, but it worries me."

"Don't worry about nothing, mija. I promise, I'm going to be careful. This is what I have to do if we want to have a good life when the baby comes. I'm going to open my own business. In the next six months, I'm going to make sure that we're taken care of. I don't want our baby in old dirty clothes living in a roach-infested shack."

"Yeah I know, but what good is all that if you get locked up?" said Angelina.

"Just trust me, ok? We are going to have a good life," I said.

"Ok, Joaquín," answered Angelina as she reached over and kissed me.

We drove to the biggest furniture store in town and picked out an entire living room set, a kitchen table with chairs and a king size bedroom set. Plans were made to have everything delivered in the evening to the apartment. Then we went to Wal-Mart and bought pans, pots, utensils, plates, bowls, cups and anything else we needed. Angelina's face was bright with wonder as I paid with hundreds. With my back seat and trunk full of bags we drove to our new apartment. Surprisingly I hadn't seen any vatos from VSL yet. As we unloaded our bags, the delivery truck with our furniture drove up into the big parking lot. This was all happening so fast. I wanted to invite my parents over so they could be proud of what I had. I wanted to tell them about the baby coming. But I knew that they wouldn't be happy for me. They would know that I made this money illegally. The delivery truck left and I placed all of the furniture where Angelina and I wanted it. Besides television and stereo, the apartment looked completely furnished. I sat and rested with Angelina and let the new apartment settle in on us. Just yesterday Angelina was at the park, thrown out of her house with nowhere to go, and now she had an entire apartment with brand new furniture.

Just as I was feeling relaxed my pager started beeping. I was startled because I had forgotten I had it. I looked at the number and it was my tió's cellular number with a 911 code. I quickly hooked up the phone into the phone jack and dialed his number. I heard his phone ring twice then he answered, "Hello!"

"It's me, Joaquín. What's going on," I said.

"I need you here now! I can't talk on this phone," he said sounding stressed.

"Ok, I'll be right over," I answered as I heard his line hang up.

"I gotta go mija, my tió needs me," I said.

"Why? I want you to stay," she said.

"I'm sorry, but he said it's important. I'll be back as soon as I can," I said as I handed her a few hundred dollar bills and the key to the front door. I was out the door before she said goodbye.

What could it be? Was my tió ok, was my tía ok? A million things ran through my mind. Was my tió in trouble or maybe the cops raided his house? I didn't have any clavo or nada so I was speeding all the way to his house. What normally takes an hour to drive I made in thirty minutes. Just as I pulled into his driveway my pager beeped again. It was my tió calling from his house. I quickly ran toward the front door and knocked. My tió opened it with a gun sticking out of his pocket.

"Come in," he said as I followed him to the family room. Four other men sat there. Some were crying in rage.

"What happened?" I asked feeling confused.

"Mi camarada.... my friend was found dead in his house this morning," he answered talking between his teeth. "DAMN IT! Somebody is going to pay!"

"Who tió... who was found dead?" I asked.

"Solario... one of the men that went to dinner with us last night. He was tortured and shot," he said now pacing back and forth.

Suddenly his cellular phone rang. He answered and it was about who did the murder.

"Ok, where does he live!" yelled my tió into his cellular phone.

My tió hung his phone up, "I know who did it! It was Juan de Culiacan. I'm going to skin him alive!" said my tió now angrier than ever.

"Let's go," he said as we all stood up. All four men were loading their guns and making sure their clips were full. One of the men was now crying uncontrollably.

"You stay here Victor... yo me encargo de esto," said my tió as he held Victor's shoulders.

"No puedo, I need to be there. I can't stay while you go out. It was my brother that was killed. Please Cuerno, let me go along," pleaded the crying man.

"Ok... ok. I'll let you come along, but you need to calm down. There is time to mourn and there is time to do what must be done."

Then my tió turned to one of the other men, "I need you

to call back to Mexico, let them know what is going on. If Juan tries to go back to Culiacán, I want men waiting for him. I want to kill him myself, even if I have to go down there myself. And call everyone we know in town. I doubt he's home. If he's still in town I want to know where he's at."

"What about me tió, what do you want me to do?" I asked.

"I want you by my side. I need familia around me, ok?"

"Ok, don't worry. I got your back," I said.

"That's what I want to hear, mijo," replied my tió.

"Well before we go, I have your money. Where do you want me to put it?" I asked.

"Give it to your tia. She's in the bedroom," he said.

"Ok."

"Hurry, I'll meet you outside," said my tió as he walked out with the other men.

I walked over to his bedroom and my tia was sitting on the bed crying. I slowly walked in as she noticed me. She quickly wiped the tears away.

"My tió told me to give this to you," I said as I handed her six thousand dollars.

"Thank you Joaquín... I'm so scared," she said now crying again.

I just stood there, not knowing what to say.

"I know I can't stop him, but... I'm so afraid one of these days he won't come back."

"I'll take care of him, tia."

She looked up at me as I stood there. "Will you? Will you make sure he comes home?" she asked desperately for an answer.

"I promise, I won't let nothing happen to him," I said.

Then I turned around and walked away. I could hear her sobbing loudly as I closed the front door behind me.

We left in two separate cars. I sat in the back seat of my tió's car as two of the other men followed in a new black Blazer. The sun was now setting and I could feel the tension in the car, like hot lava pouring, destroying everything in it's way. I pulled out my cuete from my jacket pocket and made sure it was full of bullets. I could feel my body shaking nervously, sweat collecting on my back and forehead. I thought of Angelina, glad that she didn't know what I was doing right now. I thought of my tia as she sat on the bed crying, hoping my tió would come home alive. We were now driving out into the country as my tió drove faster and faster. I could smell the peaches from the orchard fields on each side of the small country road. Finally, we drove into a small ranch as my tió popped his trunk open. We all jumped out and one of the men from the Blazer ran and kicked the front door open. I could hear voices yelling. My tió reached into his trunk and pulled out an AR-33 assault rifle, in his other hand a machete. Then, we approached the house and then ran into the house as one of my tió's men was kicking a man on the floor.

"No es Juan!" yelled one of the men to my tió.

"¿Quién eres?" my tió asked as he pointed the AR-33 to the mans throat.

"Soy Francisco... I don't know what you want," said the man with his mouth trembling with fear.

"¿Dónde esta Juan? Tell me! Or I'll kill you," said my tió as he put his finger on the trigger. My heartbeat felt as if it had stopped. The man began crying and yelling out that he didn't know where Juan was at.

"Oh, you don't know where he's at!" yelled my tió. Then he pointed his assault rifle at the man's leg and let one shot go. My nerves jumped with the loud echoing bullet sound. The bullet ripped through his leg and into the floor. The man was now screaming in pain as he held his leg. Blood was everywhere.

"I don't know where Juan is at... por favor... no me mates," begged the man on the floor.

Just then my tió's cellular phone rang. He answered, "Qué. Oh ok, which room," asked my tió as he looked blindly toward me. "Ok, I'm going right over." Then he put the phone back into his pocket. "Let's go."

The man was now crying silently and praying the rosary to himself as we walked out of the house.

We got in the car and my tió hit the gas as his wheels began spinning, and dust was flying everywhere as we got back onto the small country road. I glanced back toward the house, wondering what the shot man was going to do. We drove back and stopped at a small motel on the outskirts of town. My tió sent one of the men to the office with a wad of money. We waited for a few seconds then the man came back out with a motel key.

"Give me the key," said my tió to the man getting back into the car.

"He's in room number forty five," said the man.

We drove toward the room and parked around the corner of the building. My uncle put the AR-33 and machete in the car and left the trunk open. The two men in the Blazer parked facing the street, making sure no cops would drive by. My tió told us to stay back as he walked up to the door and slowly put the key into the keyhole. He held a huge 9mm handgun. He turned the key, looked toward us and forced the door open. He rushed in and I could hear wrestling inside. We all ran into the small motel room as my tió was forcing the man on the floor.

"Shut up!" he yelled as he hit the man on the head with his

gun.

"Let me go...What are you doing?" screamed the man.

"I said shut up! Talk again and I'll shoot you in the mouth," said my tió as he shoved his 9mm into the man's mouth. The man knew my tió was serious and stopped yelling. One of the men with us pulled out duct tape from his jacket and taped the man's hands behind his back, and then tied his legs together. My tió began lifting up the mattress and looking into the drawers. Sure enough, he found the six pounds of crank stolen from his dead friend.

"Is this what Solario's life was worth?" asked my tió as he kicked Juan in the head two times, temporarily knocking him out.

"Take these bags to the Blazer," said my tió pointing to me. I put my gun back into my pocket and grabbed all the bags and ran outside. I put them into the back seat of the Blazer. My tió followed me and talked to the driver, "Take these to your house. Then meet me at the orchard."

"Ok," said the driver as he turned the truck on and drove off. I walked back into the room, the two men were picking Juan up and carrying him to my tió's car. They threw him into the trunk and closed it. I sat back into the car as my tió started it. I could hear the man moaning and kicking the back seat. I felt sick, as if I wanted to throw up. My tió put music on to drown out the sound of the man. It was night time now. We drove toward the small foothills. There was nothing but orchards out there. As we drove on a dirt road toward the back of the orchard I could hear the man violently kicking the back seat. It was making me nervous; I knew this man was going to die. My tió's cellular rang, and it was the two men in the Blazer, letting him know that they were right behind us. Finally toward the back of the orchard was a big open space with some tractors parked.

We all got out of the car as the Blazer parked. My tió hit the button for his trunk to pop open. The man screamed as my tió punched him in the mouth. Blood splattered as his top lip busted.

"Grab him!" yelled my tió to me as we lifted him out of the trunk and threw him on the floor. One of his hands were loose from the duct tape.

"Please...please, don't kill me!" cried Juan.

"Is that what Solario said to you?... huh... answer me!" screamed my tió as he stabbed him in the stomach with the huge machete.

"Ooooooohhh... If you kill me, I swear my family is going to kill you. I swear! Your whole familia is dead!" yelled Juan as he reached for the stab wound with his free hand.

I couldn't believe this was happening. We all stood around this man as he was bleeding to death. My tió reached over to the man and stabbed him again. The man threw up blood from his mouth as his eyes widened with terror. He was trying to talk but he couldn't. He began gagging in his own blood and squealing, like a pig being butchered. It was the worst sound I had ever heard. His cries no longer sounded human. I tried to not think about it. I looked away for a second. The man was now squirming in the dirt like a dog that's been run over by a car. His feet were freed from the duct tape as he tried to stand up. He fell on his knees in front of my tió.

"Before you die, I want you to know this... your wife, your kids, your mother, and father will all be dead in Culiacán before this night ends," said my tió very calmly.

"I'll see you con el diablo in hell!" said the man as he spits blood in my tió's face.

Before my tió could react, I pulled out my cuete and shot the man in his chest. He fell to the ground. The shot didn't kill him, he was still moving. I suddenly thought of Vince and of the pain, my tió must be feeling. Rage came over me, so I bent down toward the man and pistol-whipped him. I wanted to see more blood. I wanted to see blood for my tió's friend. I wanted to see blood for Vince. I felt hands pulling me away from Juan. I could feel blood on my face as I looked at my blood soaked hands. Then it felt like a dream, and I wondered if I was really there. Was I really here? Was this really happening? I was drunk with anger as my uncle began to hack at the man with his machete. The man screamed one last time then became silent. The only sound was of the machete cutting through meat and bone.

I couldn't stop the tears as they ran down my face. I just wanted to be numb, not wanting to feel anything. I sat back as the men began to dig a hole with shovels they had in the Blazer. Once the hole was dug the men pushed the corpse in. Parts of his arms and legs were also thrown in with him. My tió took his shovel and smashed his teeth and face in. I couldn't help it as I gagged and threw up everything I ate that day. No one would ever report this man missing. No one would ever go to the cops. He didn't even have any papers proving that he lived in the United States. And to think this happened all of the time, when necessary.

The shovels were thrown back into the Blazer and the four men left. My tió and I got into his car and also drove off. No words were said as we drove through the country with the windows down.

"We gotta clean up," said my tió as we pulled into the driveway of one of his houses. It was the house where all the crank and marijuana was.

"Stay here," said my tió as he got out of the car and knocked on the front door. A man opened the door and quickly gave my tió a set of keys. He motioned for me to follow him as he walked to the back of the house. I stepped out and followed him to a small guest house in the back.

"Go in the restroom and take a shower. Throw me your clothes so I can burn them," said my tió. "I'm going to send my friend here to get some clothes for us. Give me your pants, shirt, socks... everything. Even your shoes."

"Ok," I said as I went into the restroom and undressed. I looked in the mirror and I saw blood smeared all over my body. I did as he said and threw all the clothes outside of the door. As I stepped into the shower I looked down at my feet. The water was red as it ran down the drain. I made sure all of the blood was washed off. I stood there and let the water hit my face. It had been a night I'd never forget. As I turned the water off I could hear my tió talking, I guessed to the man that lived here.

"Here are some clothes!" yelled my tió through the door. I slightly opened the door as he handed me the clothes to wear. Most of it was baggy but it would do. I stepped out, as my tió walked in. He did the same as me, throwing his clothes outside the door so it could be burned. The man had a fire going outside of the small guest house. He grabbed my tió's clothes and tossed it into the fire. Then the man washed the dust from my tió's car with a water hose. The guest home was a one bedroom, small kitchen and living room house. I sat at the kitchen table as I waited for my tió. After a few minutes, he stepped out and sat down next to me on the table.

"Look mijo, it will be ok... But I want to ask you a question... why did you become so wild? You didn't even know Solario," said my tió. "What I did to Juan had to be done. Are you upset because of what I had to do?"

"No, that's not the problem. I'm sorry, it's just something else. I know that what you did had to be done," I said.

"I know that I've taught you how to sell this trabajo, and I've taught you how to weight it, too. But you have to know about this other part of la vida, mijo. In this life, you can never, ever let anybody get over on you. Believe me, they will take your kindness as a weakness. You have to let everyone know that you mean business, or else they will walk all over you. I know how your barrio fights other barrios, your enemies are very clear. You know who you're against and who's your homeboy. But in this vida, you can never know. Don't ever trust anyone one hundred percent, because the second you do, you've already lost," explained my tió.

"Tió... I just want you to know that you can always trust me. You have done so much for me in such little time. I feel as if I've known you my entire life. I will do anything for you, tió," I said truly feeling close to this man. This man I had just met, but I felt love for him. Without his help, I would have been homeless with Angelina. We gave each other a big abrazo and walked outside. My tió popped his trunk open and put his AR-33 into the small shed where all of the crank and marijuana was.

As we neared my tió's house he turned to me and said, "I don't ever want to talk about this night."

"I know tió, I wish I could forget it," I said as we pulled into the driveway. We got out of the car and walked into the house. My tia was still awake sitting on the couch by herself. She quickly stood up and ran toward my tió, hugging him. I didn't say anything as I walked up the steps to my room and let myself drop on the bed. I was so exhausted that I fell asleep with all of my clothes on. I didn't even bother to pull the sheets back. That night I had dreams of Juan screaming as my tió hacked him with the machete. In my dre,am he wouldn't die. He just screamed and screamed.

———————

12

The next morning I was awakened by knocking at the door.

"Hey, Joaquín. Wake up," said my tió.

"Huh," I said trying to figure out who it was, still in a deep sleep.

"It's me, your tió. Get up, I need to talk to you."

"Ok, I'm coming," I said half asleep as I opened the door to the bedroom.

"Mijo, I need you to go back to your barrio for a few days. One of the cops in town is a friend of mine. He called me and said that someone reported a fight at the motel. I got the six pounds that were stolen from Solario's. Thdownstairsstairs. I need you to sell two of them to one of Solario's customers right now. All you have to do is meet him downtown by the bus station. He's going to pay you ten thousand for both of them. Bring me all of the money and I'll let you keep the other four pounds. I'm going to use those ten thousand dollars to pay for Solario's funeral. I don't want you to come back for at least seven days," said my tió as he stood in the doorway. "Nobody is going to be selling anything. Detectives are investigating Solario's death. The whole town is being shaken down, and they are looking for the murderer."

"What time is it?" I asked looking out of my window. It was still dark out.

"It's six in the morning. El hombre espera."

I woke up and didn't bother taking a shower. I brushed my teeth and ran downstairs.

"The libras are already in your bumper. just go down the street all the way and you'll see the Greyhound station," he said.

"Ok, I'll be right back," I said as I got into my car and drove off.

I found the bus station quick and easy. A man in a brand new Bronco stepped out.

"Are you here for Cuerno?" asked the man.

"Simón, I brought something for you," I said reaching into my back bumper and pulling out the huge package.

"Tell Cuerno that I'm sorry about Solario," said the man as he handed me a roll of cash.

"Orale, I'll let him know," I said as I put the wad of money in my pocket. I didn't feel like making small talk so I shook his hand and got back into my ranfla. I drove back up into the driveway as my tió walked out. He had all four pounds packaged with duct tape as he put them all one by one into my bumper. The sun was beginning to rise.

"I'm going to grab some clothes," I said as I walked back into the house. I ran upstairs and grabbed enough clothes for the week, making sure I had my cuete with me.

"I'll page you if I need you ok, mijo? And call me if you got any problems."

"Are you going to be ok?" I asked.

"Don't worry about me, nothing is going to happen," said my tió.

"Orale pues tió. I'll be calling ok?" I said as I put my car in drive and drove off. The morning traffic had the freeway full, and I looked as if I was just going to work. It was a firme time to have clavo with me. I had always liked the early mornings, the air smelling fresh as the sun came up. I drove the speed limit all the way back to Barrio Apache. I felt relieved as I drove in the apartment parking lot. Once again I had made it with no problems from cops. I put the four pounds inside a paper bag I had sitting in my trunk. With clothes in hand and the bag, I knocked on the apartment door.

I knocked for what seemed like a minute when I heard Angelina walking toward the door.

"Who is it?" she asked from the inside.

"It's me, Joaquín," I said in a whisper. I didn't want to wake up the neighbors. The door opened immediately.

"Joaquín! Come in, is everything ok?" she asked as I walked into the apartment.

She closed the door behind me as I sat on the couch.

"Yes, everything is fine, mija. I just wanted to come to see you."

I sat on the couch remembering Juan de Culiacán, my tió, the machete and of the hole they put him in. I couldn't get it out of my head. I still felt as if his blood was all over me. What the hell was I getting myself into? Whether I liked it or not, the money was too good to stop now.

"JOAQUIN!"

"Yeah, what mija?" I answered startled by the loudness of her voice.

"I've been calling your name for the past minute. What's

wrong?" Angelina asked as she sat down next to me.

"Oh, I'm just tired I guess. I'm going to lay down… I'm still sleepy," I said as I stood up and walked to the bedroom. I took my clothes and shoes off and laid down in my boxers. I could feel Angelina lay down next to me as I fell asleep.

I had a dream that Angelina was in labor. We were at the hospital waiting for the baby to come. I felt excited as the nurses and doctor were getting everything ready for the baby. Angelina was breathing hard and pushing. I felt nervous and excited. It was going to be a brand new life for me. I could hear the baby monitor beeping with the baby's heartbeat. And just before the baby was coming out the doctor turned to me, eyes wide open. It was Juan, screaming. He was screaming with no sound and tried to strangle me. I fought him away, but I felt weak.

"No… noooo!" I yelled as I jumped up out of bed full of sweat. "Joaquín… It's me, it's me baby," I heard Angelina say as she held me. I laid back down breathing hard. I looked at her to make sure I wasn't dreaming anymore. It took me a minute to finally calm down.

"What happened to you last night?" asked Angelina.

"Nothing I ever want to talk about. Please don't ever ask me again," I said as I stood up and walked into the bathroom to take a shower. Once I finished taking a shower I felt rested up. I ironed got ready and sat down in the kitchen. It was now ten thirty in the morning. Angelina took a shower and also sat down at the table with me. We ate breakfast together. I called Big Ed and let him know that I was back in town for a few days. I asked him to stop by in a couple of hours. Angelina and I sat there and talked about the baby, which helped me take my mind off of the night before. Within an hour Big Ed showed up with money for one pound of crank. He already had the money for it, paying me five thousand for it. It was all profit since my tió gave the four pounds to me.

Once Big Ed left I took Angelina to an electronic store and bought an entertainment center with t.v., VCR and surround sound. It was scheduled to be delivered the next morning. I couldn't help but call my tió on his cellular to make sure everything was firme. He said that everything was fine, but he still didn't want to do anything for a few days.

Angelina and I drove by my parents house. I wanted to stop. It took all of my strength to not stop and say hi to them. Angelina noticing how I was feeling asked, "Why don't you stop? I'm sure they'd be happy to see you."

"I don't know... my dad don't want me around his chante," I said.

"He's your dad no matter what. He's not going to slam the door in your face," answered Angelina.

"He don't want me around. He said that I'm nothing but trouble. If VSL sees my car parked in front, they might try to do something," I said as I drove on past the house.

The next day I called Big Ed and told him to get Chuey, Alfredo, Dragon, Spider, Crow and Tobo at the park. I wanted to talk to them about making feria. I drove back to the apartment and dropped Angelina off. I let her know that I was going to the park to talk business with the homeboys.

On the way to the park, I was thinking of how I wanted to make them a part of my business. I wanted Apache to be on top of things. I wanted Barrio Apache to control this entire town. As I drove up to the park Big Ed was already there sitting in the shade with the homies. The park was full of twisted old trees and broken bottles. I walked up and shook all of their hands, then I sat down with them.

"I'm glad you vatos came out here today. I wanted to finish

our conversation we had the other day at the burrito stand," I said as I looked at each of the homeboys.

"What did you mean when you said that it's going to be different now?" asked Dragon.

"What I mean is that it's time to make feria. Do you like looking for change to get a taco? Do you like walking everywhere cause you can't afford a ranfla?" I asked.

"Hell no, Chale. I want to have things," replied Chuey.

"Serio, ese, I'm sick of being broke!" Dragon said excitedly.

"Ok then, look. I got hooked up with a good connect for bud and crank. I get it at such a good price that we can all make money. I can get pounds at a time and break them up into ounces and half ounces. Then you can sell them to whoever you know around town," I said.

"Well, how much are you talking about ese? I don't want to do it unless I make good feria. I don't want to get busted for a few twenty dollar bills," said Chuey.

"I can give you ounces for three hundred and fifty dollars each. I know for a fact that you can sell that same ounce for five or six hundred. You don't want to break it down smaller than that. If each of you had two people to buy ounces from you every few days then you would make some good feria. You could easily make five or six hundred a week," I said.

"Damn loco, now that's what I'm talking about!" said Tobo as he reached over and shook my hand.

"Hell yeah ese, what are we waiting for!" yelled Dragon.

"And in a short time homies, we'll be on top of this town. Like I said, each of you need two people to buy ounces every few days. And don't ever get tempted to break it down. You don't want to make yourselves hot. Let your dealers be out in the street with the tweakers. That way, all you have to worry about is your two dealers. If you get snitched on, then you know exactly who told on you. We need total control of who has what and who is doing what," I said now standing up.

"Damn loco, what got into you?" asked Chuey.

"...Somebody just helped me see things clearly... In time we will be so powerful that VSL will never be able to stand up against us," I said now talking loudly.

"Orale, like you said vato. It's time for a new Barrio Apache," said Tobo.

"Simón," we all said as we shook hands Chicano style.

"Here's my pager number. I just got a place with Angelina. I don't want anybody going over, so I'm sorry about that. Nobody can know where this stuff is coming from. So as soon as you got someone to buy something from you, just page me and I'll call you right back," I said.

We all kicked back joking around for a while, I almost felt normal again. So much had happened to me in such a small amount of time. I went to jail, I was kicked out of my house, Angelina was kicked out of her house, I met my tió, I learned how to sell drugs and I helped torture and kill a man. I felt as if I were years older. I knew that if I could get through this for the next six months, I could get through anything.

Sure enough within a week all of the homeboys found people to sell too. Big Ed sold two of the pounds and the last pound I broke down into sixteen ounces. It only took a week for the last pound to sell. I had a full profit of over twenty thousand dollars stashed inside my apartment. My tió called and said it was ok to start the business up again. I didn't want to move back with him, so I had to travel a lot to where he was.

Things were going so good after a month that I bought a brand new Lincoln Town car, paid in cash. Life was good, other than a few fist fights with vatos from VSL. It seemed like we didn't have enough time to waste with them. We didn't go to their barrio's looking for trouble anymore. As long as we kept them out of Apache, we didn't care what they were doing. As a matter of fact, most of them got addicted to crank. We had neutral vatos that didn't claim going into the VSL barrio and selling them crank all day long. I didn't keep anything at my house either; it was too risky. I would only bring what I needed to bring for Big Ed and the homeboys. Instead of giving the homies ounces at a time, I would just give them each quarter pounds. That way I was only making a trip once a week. I was also selling the marijuana to Black each week. But instead of transporting it all into town, I would have him drive closer to the town my tió lived in. Money couldn't have been made easier. It seemed like I was making money faster than I could spend it.

Angelina was getting bigger as the months passed. I also bought her a brand new Honda Accord, with rims and tinted windows. She only hung around my homies ladies. Things were going along smoothly. All of the homeboys were living good now. We would meet in restaurants out of town. That way the cops wouldn't see us all of the time in these nice places. I loved to see the look on the waitresses faces when we would all walk in to eat. I'm sure we all looked like we were going to rob the place. Chuey with his arms full of tattoos and Tobo with a pafio on his head. Never would I have thought that I would be sitting in restaurants with the homies from Barrio Apache, fighting over who's going to pay the bill. They all wanted to prove to each other that they were making more money that the other.

A month later Chuey got a violation for probation and was put in jail for driving without a license. Crow stabbed a vato from VSL and was sentenced to a year in la pinta. We all made sure their books were full at all times. Chuey did thirty days in jail and went back to business the day he got out. I hired my tió's lawyer for the case I had pending. All charges against me were eventually dropped for not having sufficient evidence. They couldn't prove a thing, so I was free. It made me laugh when I walked into court with a lawyer. The judges in this town had never had a Chicano take a big time lawyer and fight. The lawyer had the D.A. stuttering with nothing to say.

As each week passed, I would pick up crank from my tió. I would also ask him quesTións about his record business. I was slowly saving money so I could have a good jump start once the baby was born. I found out more about how my tió was so connected. My tfa's familia in Mexico was one of the biggest dealers in the state of Michoacdn. My tfa Isabel moved to the United States to get away from the life of her family. She met my Tió and they were married within a year. Once her familia saw how determined and ruthless my tió could be, they let him into the family business.

Within four months I was introduced to all of my tió's crew, vatos that worked for him. Every dealer needed a crew, guys they could trust with their life. My crew consisted of the homeboys from Apache, Big Ed, Dragon, Tobo, Spider and my primo Alfredo. We all watched each others backs. But of all the people I was introduced to, the most important was Don Chavelfn Sanchez, Isabel's father. I met him at my tió's house when he made a quick trip to visit his daughter, my tfa. The second he walked into my tió's house you could feel his presence. He was an averaged sized man with eyes that made you shiver. I wondered how many men felt the wrath of this man. I shook his hand in respect and couldn't help but notice a huge diamond ring on his pinky finger. I would have guessed that Don Chavelfn Sanchez had never smiled in his life, until Isabel walked into the living room where we were sitting. He quickly stood up and hugged Isabel, kissing her hands and cheek. He was a tough man, but when it came to Isabel I could see that his cold heart melted. He even cried because he said that Isabel looked exactly like her mother. She had died ten years ago.

Angelina was now seven months pregnant. I didn't want to tell Angelina, but I liked this life. Why would I be stupid and quit this life of power and luxury when the baby was born? In time I could own ranches in Mexico. I could own land in the United States, businesses and houses. Besides, my nightmares of Juan had stopped by now.

And our power in town was greater than ever. No one dared come against us. Every single dealer in town now bought from me or my crew. A few argued a little, but with a little threat or push, they all eventually bought from us. It was either work for us or get shut down. No one could compete with our prices. I had to admit, this life was good and nothing was going to stop me.

13

Angelina had less than a month to go. I now had over a hundred thousand dollars hidden in the apartment, and that didn't count for the thousands of dollars I spent on furniture, cars, and clothes. Everything was like clockwork. I transported all of the crank and weed, broke it all down into ounces for the homeboys and gave Big Ed a few pounds a week. I also sold twenty pounds of weed to Black every five or six days.

"Joaquín," said Angelina as she sat on the couch massaging her large round belly.

"Yeah mija, do you need anything?" I asked as I sat down next to her.

"I want to talk to you... we need to talk."

"What's up, is something wrong?" I asked concerned.

"Well... I know that I told you that I wouldn't ask you about your business. But... I think you should quit now. Why wait until the baby is born? You already made enough money."

"What are you talking about? Don't you realize how much money I bring in a week How the hell am I going to stop just like that? You agreed with me that you wouldn't ask me my business," I said sharply.

"I'm tired of not saying anything. This isn't about you anymore, this is about us. You, me and this baby. I'm not going to lie, I love to have money. But what good is all of this if you aren't around! You said that your doing it so we could have things, so the baby could have a better life. But it's all gonna go down the drain if something happens to you," said Angelina, trying to reason with me.

"I can't believe you're telling me all of this. Nothing is going to happen. Money is coming in better than ever. My tió has been doing this for years, and you don't see him dead or in jail. I know what I'm doing."

"Are you saying that you aren't going to stop when our baby is born?" asked Angelina, by now shaken and angry.

"Look, I changed my plans. I don't see any reason to stop. I've made so much money this past year. Imagine how much I can make in the next five years, or ten years."

"Joaquín, listen to yourself!"

"I didn't do all of this so you could turn against me!" I yelled.

"I'm not turning against you, I'm just afraid. I have dreams that you never make it to the hospital when I'm in labor, and..."

"Don't talk like that! Nothing is going to stop me from being there. Don't you ever say that again!" I said.

Angelina began to cry as she slowly stood up and walked to the bedroom. I couldn't believe she was saying all of these things. She had nothing before this, and now she had everything. I grabbed my keys from my kitchen table and walked out of the door. I wanted to see how Big Ed was doing. All of my crew had pagers and cellular phones. That way we could keep in touch with each other at all times. I called Big Ed and let him know that I was on my way to his new house. He had moved out of his parents and now rented a new two-story house.

Big Ed was sitting in the shade on his front yard as I drove into his driveway.

"¿Qué onda vato?" said, Big Ed, as we shook hands.

"Nada, I just wanted to come to kick it for a minute. Angelina's trippin on me, so I didn't feel like sticking around," I said as I sat down on the soft grass.

"Well homie, you can kick it here for as long as you want," he said.

"Orale, I'll just need to calm down for a couple hours," I told him.

We talked and joked for about an hour, then my pager beeped. It was my tió paging me from his cellular. I called right back.

"What's up tió?" I asked.

"Hey, I got some important business. I want to know if you're interested," asked my tió.

"Well... tell me what this business is about," I asked.

"Ya sabes, no hablo de negocios en el telefono. Can you come down right now?" he asked.

"Yeah, I'll be right there. Give me about an hour," I said as I hung the phone up.

"What happened?" asked Big Ed as I stood up to leave.

"I don't know. My tió wants me to go down there right now," I answered.

"Is it something bad?"

"I don't know homie, I can never tell with my tió," I said as I got into my car and drove off.

The drive didn't seem so long anymore. Going to my tió's at least once a week became common. I began to feel a little guilty for yelling at Angelina. I shouldn't have yelled at her. It wasn't her fault for worrying. I knew that I had planned on stopping as soon as the baby was born. But if everything was going good, why would I stop? With only a couple weeks before the baby was due, I felt pressured to not stop selling. I couldn't help but feel as if I was in a race against time. I parked and walked up to my tió's walkway. My tia opened the door after I knocked and let me in.

"What's up tió?" I asked as I sat in the living room with him. He was staring at his aquarium.

"We got a problem, mijo. It's a serious problem," he said now focusing on me.

I sat back on the couch and relaxed, waiting to hear what he had to say.

"Don Chavelin Sanchez called me this morning. Isabel's brother Jorge, was robbed of a half million dollar deal a few nights ago. Over a hundred pounds of crank and some cash were taken at gunpoint," explained my tió as he stood up and began pacing.

"What does that have to do with us?" I asked.

"Well, he just found out that the man that did it fled to the United States, and that he has reason to believe that the man is hiding in your town. Jorge had done business with him before and remembered that he had familia in the U.S. Well... he called and wanted me to ask you if you could... find this man."

"Simón I'll find him, especially if Don Chavelfn Sanchez asked me," I said excitedly that the Don would consider me to do a job for him.

"He figures that the money is gone, but... he wants that man dead, it's the principle of it. Mijo, you don't have to do this if you don't want too. I know how you felt when we did what we had to do to Juan de Culiacan. And..."

"Look tió, I don't care about what happened to Juan. That was months ago, don't judge me by that. If Don Chavelin asked this of me, then I'm going to do it. The man that gains it all is the man that's willing to risk it all, ¿Qué no?"

"Your right Joaquín..." said my tió in deep thought, nodding his head. "Here is the man's picture. His name is Lencho, and he's thirty-five years old. He's skinny with long hair. Don't take his small size as a weakness; he's a very ruthless man. He might be expecting someone from Mexico to come looking for him. That's why Don Chavelin Sanchez wants you to find him. You have a different look, you're young. Most of the men in this business aren't cholos. If you approach him, he will never suspect that Don Chavelfn sent someone as young as you. Lencho could sense someone like me from a mile away," said my tió.

"Ok, give me the picture and tell Don Chavelin Sanchez that the man will be a memory within the week," I said as I took the picture.

"I'm sure Don Chavelin will be pleased, mijo. But I want you to be careful," said my tió as I stood up to leave.

"Don't worry about me tió, I've learned from the best," I said as we gave each other a big abrazo.

"You're a fine man Joaquín, and you have the heart of a thousand men."

"Gracias. I'll see you in a few days," I said as I drove off back toward Barrio Apache.

I was on a mission and I'd waste no time. I stopped at Big Ed's chante. I needed his help in finding this man. I didn't want anyone else involved, not even the rest of the homeboys. This was a very serious subject, and the fewer vatos involved the better. Throughout the months we had collected guns and assault rifles and kept them in a storage rental. It was rented under someone else's name so no one could trace it if we ever got busted. We had two AK-47's, one Mac-90, an AR-15, and five 9mm Glocks.

I knew that if this man was hiding in town he would be trying to move the stolen crank, probably in the local Mexican bars and restaurants. We each took one of the 9mm Glocks to carry as we drove around town looking for the man. The bar most commonly known for small drug deals was called El Sinaloa bar located on the outskirts of town. We parked as Big Ed walked inside to use the restroom. He was never carded because he looked older and he knew the bartender. I waited as I looked at each man coming out or going in. I swore that I was going to make an example of this man. Stealing from Don Chavelin was like stealing from my tio. Big Ed now walked out and walked towards the car.

"Let me see that picture again," asked Big Ed grinning.

"¿Qué Is he in there?" I asked.

"Simón, that's him," said Big Ed as he looked at the picture.

"Was he drunk?" I asked.

"Looks like he's getting there," answered Big Ed.

"Orale, let's just wait here and see where he goes," I said.

It was now night time and as we waited, cars came and went. The bar was going to close in a few minutes when we saw Lencho walk out and get into an older Cadillac. After a few minutes, he drove off toward town as we followed him in a distance. He parked in a small apartment complex and walked up to a door and knocked. A man opened the door and let him in. We waited for a few more minutes, then he walked back out.

"What the hell is he doing?" asked Big Ed.

"I thought he lived there, but maybe that's where he hid the crank," I said.

"He's getting back in the car," said Big Ed pointing to Lencho. I turned the car on and followed him toward the country. I didn't follow close behind because in the country there were no other cars. We would be noticed very quickly. We slowly passed where Lencho had stopped. Through the window, we could see women in the house. "It must be his family's house," I said.

"Orale, now what?" asked Big Ed.

"Let's just go back home, tomorrow we'll get the guns out of storage and kill this vato," I said.

"Cool," Big Ed replied as we drove back toward his house. I dropped him off and drove to my apartment.

Angelina was still awake watching TV.

"Joaquin!" said Angelina as she stood up to hug me.

"Hi, mija," I said as I sat down on the couch.

"I'm sorry about earlier," said Angelina as she sat back down.

"So am I. I didn't mean to argue with you," I said.

"I love you Joaquín. I'm so worried. It was getting late and your cellular was off. I thought something happened to you," said Angelina.

"I'm ok, I'm home. I had to visit with my tió and I got back late," I said.

She hugged me tenderly and we went to the bedroom. I took a shower and relaxed. Tomorrow was going to be a busy day. But no matter how busy or hectic my day was, being home with Angelina always made me feel better. She became more beautiful the closer the due date came. Maybe she was right that I should quit selling. After all, I had enough money to start my record company. It couldn't be too hard to find

Chicano rappers to put out. I knew I had all the know how to start in the record business, from distributors and manufacturing to promotions.

Once we were in bed I pulled her closer to me.

"I love you, baby," I whispered to her. I could see her eyes shining with the moonlight coming through the bedroom window. "There is nowhere else I'd rather be right now."

"I love you too, Joaquín. You're everything to me," said Angelina.

"I thought about what you've told me! and... after tomorrow I'm going to quit. I have something really important to do, but after that, I'm done," I said.

"Really!" asked Angelina excitedly.

"Yes, really. No more dealing," I answered.

Angelina hugged me tighter as we began to kiss. I held her close to me as we made love. It wasn't the same as always. It felt more intense. Telling her I would quit and really meaning it took a huge weight off me. It felt as if we were the only two people in the world. I forgot about my deals, my money, my power, and my homies. This is what it was all about, being with someone that cared about you. I slowly kissed her body, her lips. I felt closer to her than I ever had as I softly touched her pregnant belly.

"I feel so close to you, Joaquín," whispered Angelina in my ear. "I never want this to end." She put her hand on mine as I rubbed her belly, trying to feel the baby move. I pushed all thoughts away of what I had to do tomorrow.

The next day I woke up with mixed feelings. I knew that I wanted to quit, but I still had business to take care of. If all I had to do was kill Lencho before I was out, then I was going to make sure he was dead and forgotten. Angelina woke up happier than I had ever seen her. She made breakfast and we ate together. I slowly ironed a black pair of Dickies and a black shirt. I took a shower and got dressed as Angelina cleaned the apartment.

"I'll be back tonight. Don't stay up waiting, ok," I said.

"Be careful," Angelina said as she hugged me tightly, "Thank you for your decision... I'm proud of you."

"Ok, mija. I'll be back tonight," I said as I walked out. It tripped me out that she said she was proud of me. I wished my father was still proud of me. I thought of how I felt the day he looked at me with shame. I thought my entire world was going to end when he told me that he was ashamed of me. All I ever wanted was to make my father proud. I don't know what went wrong. My life became a twisted road.

I picked up Big Ed and headed to the storage rentals to pick some guns up. I choose to carry the Mac-90 assault rifle. I liked how the shots came out smooth and fast. It had two thirty round clips taped to each other. Once the clip was empty I would pop it out and flip it upside down for the other clip to pop in. Big Ed grabbed one of the AK-47's and dusted it off. Then we each grabbed two boxes of ammo we had stored in a small drawer. We hid them in the trunk and drove to Big Ed's chante.

Once we parked in the garage we closed the garage door. We pulled the guns out of the trunk and walked into the house. Big Ed lived by himself, so we didn't have to worry about anyone bothering us. We sat at the kitchen table as I made sure all of the gun parts were well oiled and ready. Then I filled each clip with bullets.

"This vato is going to wish he had never crossed Don Chavelin Sanchez. I'm gonna put the hurt in this vato," I said as I finished filling the clip.

"Simón, ese. We're gonna show fools how we do it in Barrio

Apache," said Big Ed as we shook hands.

"Orale, that's right homie. Puro Barrio Apache hasta la muerte. Nosotros controlamos todo, por vida!" I said.

"Now all we gotta do is wait. We know where he drinks, where he lives and what he drives. Tonight that vato is going to die," said Big Ed.

We waited until dark at Big Ed's chante. Then we walked out to his garage and put the guns back into the trunk. We drove straight to the bar, hoping he would be there. We slowly pulled into the parking lot and looked at all the cars, and sure enough, his ranfla was there. We sat and waited for over two hours when we saw him coming out, he was alone.

"Time to rock & roll, ese," said Big Ed very seriously.

"Here, vato. You drive." I said as I stepped out of the car and walked around to ride shotgun. "Follow him and at a stop sign I'm going to jump in his car," I said.

"Are you crazy, ese? What are you going to do?" asked Big Ed surprised.

"Don't even trip, just follow where he drives," I said.

"Ok, vato," said Big Ed as we pulled out of the parking lot and onto the street.

We followed him as he drove toward his house in the country. There was a stop sign coming up a half mile away. I felt my heart jumping out of my chest, as I knew that this was it.

"Pass him up! Then at the stop sign, I'm going to jump out. Then I'm gonna make him pass you up, just follow where ever he goes," I said now feeling the adrenaline pumping in my body.

"Orale, but stay trucha."

"Simón, I have a kid to raise," I said calmly.

Big Ed passed Lencho and stopped at the stop sign. Just as Big

Ed made a complete stop I jumped out of the seat. Lencho must have been drunk, for his actions were slow. I ran back toward his car, and he saw me coming and tried reaching under his seat. I knew that most likely he was packing a cuete. Just as I opened his passenger side door he pulled his cuete out. A loud shot rang out as his windshield cracked. I hit him on the side of his head with the butt of the 9mm Glock I was carrying. Blood ran down his face, and I could tell it dazed him. I cocked the gun back and pointed it to his head. Then I took his gun and pulled the clip out.

"¿Que quieres? What do you want with me," said Lencho in a high pitched voice.

"Drive! If you make a move I'll put a bullet into your fat head!" I said.

"I don't even know you," he now said sounding aggravated.

"It doesn't matter if you know me or not. Now drive!" I yelled. I put the barrel to his head. He passed Big Ed and drove in the direction I told him to drive.

"You're doing this to the wrong man. If you let me go now, I won't kill you," said Lencho. Blood was still dripping down his face.

"Listen Lencho... if you don't shut up and drive, I'm going to shoot you in the eye," I said now feeling angry.

"How do you know my name?" said Lencho now knowing that I meant business.

"Pull off into that field," I said.

"For what?"

"Do it!" I said.

"Ok, ok. Just don't shoot me!" yelled Lencho.

"Drive down that dirt road all the way to the back," I said as I pointed to a corner of the field. The delta aqueduct ran alongside the field. It was a huge concrete embankment with deep water. Every year cars were found, most were stolen. Sometimes bodies were found in the trunks of the cars.

"Ok, stop here," I said.

Lencho hit my gun with his elbow making me shoot through the roof of the car. He opened his door and ran out. Big Ed was still in my ranfla, but when he saw Lencho running off, he chased him, hitting him with the car and making him stumble over. Lencho rolled several times from the impact of the car. He tried to get up as I ran out after him, knowing that I couldn't let him get away.

"Where do you think you're going?" I said as I ran up to where he was laying. I aimed and shot his leg.

"Aaaaaarrrrgggg," screamed Lencho, clinching his leg as blood streamed out.

"I'm tired of playing games with you. Where's the money and the crank!" I demanded.

"What crank? What money?" said Lencho, acting as if he didn't know what I was talking about.

"I said don't play games!" then I let another shot off into his other leg. Big Ed walked up and put duct tape over his mouth, then dragged him by his legs toward the aqueduct. His head was being dragged through dirt and rocks. He was kicking trying to get away, and wincing from the gunshots to both of his legs. I walked over to my ranfla and pulled out both assault rifles. Lencho laid there, and I could see the pain in his eyes. I slapped the clip in and loaded the Mac-90.

"Listen, I'm only going to ask you once. Where is Don Chavelin's feria and crank? Your lucky we're in the U.S., cuz if this was Mexico, you'd be dead already. When I take this tape off your mouth, you better tell me where it's at. I don't want to hear you deny it, or act all stupid like you don't know what I'm talking about. If you don't tell me where it's at, I'm not gonna kill you, but your gonna wish you were dead," I said.

I reached over and yanked the duct tape from his mouth. Then I pointed the Mac-90 to his stomach area. "Now tell me!" I demanded.

"I have most of the money in my car... most of the crank is sold. I keep it all in an apartment. I have some friends there selling it for me," he quickly said.

"Do you have any money at your house? I know where you live. I'll go in there and kick that door down!" I said.

"No, no... please don't do that. My sister lives there with her daughters. Please... take my keys, the money is stuffed into the spare tire."

"Check the trunk, ese," I said to Big Ed who was standing next to the cars.

"You'd better not be lying," I said.

Big Ed opened the trunk and pulled the spare tire out. He cut into it with his pocket knife and it was full of hundred dollar bills. I turned around facing Lencho, "Tell me where the money for the crank is at, where is it hidden in the apartment?" I asked.

"If you take me there, I'll get it for you," he said.

"Hmmm, I got a better idea..." Then I hesitated for a second then said, " I'll just get it myself."

Then I aimed toward Lencho's chest and said, "Don't ever think you can get away from Don Chavelin Sanchez."

"NO!" screamed Lencho as I pulled the trigger and let the entire clip empty out on his chest and face. Big Ed just stood there, surprised. I stood there for a second, but it seemed like hours. Now it was done, finished. From this point on I could live a normal life. I looked down at Lencho's ripped body, half of his face missing. My heartbeat felt calmed, not tense anymore.

"We gotta hide the body, ese," said Big Ed.

"Bring his car over here, we'll put him in the trunk," I said. Big Ed backed Lencho's car up, then put the corpse into the trunk. Our hands were full of blood as we shut the trunk. Blood was everywhere and on the ground where Lencho laid. We kicked rocks and dirt over the blood stains until you couldn't notice anything. Then we drove the car to the edge of the aqueduct and put the Cadillac in neutral. We pushed it into the water and watched it slowly sink to the bottom. I reached down toward the water and washed most of the blood off.

"Now what, ese?" asked Big Ed.

"This isn't finished... we gotta get that feria from that apartment," I said.

"You said that Don Chavelfn wanted him dead. He didn't say anything about getting his feria back," said Big Ed.

"If I know where the money is at, why would I not finish this? I really appreciate you helping me out with this, but you don't have to go with me if you don't want," I said.

"It's not like that, vato. I'm down with you por vida. If you want to get that feria, then I'm with you."

"Orale, I'll make it worthwhile for you, homie. I knew that I could count on you," I said as we walked back to my car and drove back into town.

"When we get to the apartment, I'll knock. You just back me up. If they ask me who I am, I'm going to tell them I'm looking for Lencho. As soon as they crack the door open, I'm going to force the door open. I'll hold em at gun point while you get the money. I'll force them to hand it over, even if I got to beat it out of em," I said.

"Sounds like a plan," said Big Ed as we neared the apartment.

I reached under my seat and pulled out two brown pafios so we could cover our faces. We didn't want to be recognized by anyone. I parked the ranfla a block away in a dark side street. "You ready?" I asked as I opened my trunk and pulled the two assault rifles out. I flipped the clip over. I still had a full thirty round clip. This was going to be easy. My tió was going to be proud of me, I thought.

"Let's do this," said Big Ed as we began to walk down the sidewalk. Large trees kept the moon light from shining through to the street. We reached the apartment door, and I could hear the television playing. I signaled to Big Ed to stay back and be ready. I put the pafio over my face, covering my nose and mouth. Then I looked around to the apartments and knocked.

"Who is it?" asked a woman's voice.

"Soy amigo de Lencho. Can I come in?" I asked.

"Lencho isn't here right now," answered the voice.

I knocked again, this time more aggressive. "I need to talk to Lencho!" I said.

"He isn't here," yelled a man's voice this time. Then I heard him opening the lock. As soon as he began to open the door I kicked it open, sending him flying to the floor. I rushed in holding my assault rifle at the man and women. Big Ed rushed in right after me.

"Who else is here?" I said as I aimed at the mans face.

"Nobody, just us," answered the man, shaken with fear.

"Where is the money at? If I ask you again, I'm going to kill both of you. I know Lencho keeps his money here," I demanded.

"Leave! We don't know what you are talking about!" screamed the woman.

"Shut up! Keep your damn mouth shut before I bust your

teeth in," yelled Big Ed now pointing his rifle at the woman.

"Make me shut up! Do you think I'm scared of you?" challenged the woman.

"Stop, please don't hurt my wife," begged the man.

"Why are you scared of them?" said the woman to her husband.

I turned my rifle over and swung the butt of my rifle at the mans face. His jaw collapsed as blood came running down his nose like a waterfall.

"Everytime you open your fat mouth, your husband is going to pay for it," I said pointing at the women. I was pissed. She was making this harder than it had to be.

The man was now pointing toward the kitchen. Big Ed walked over and opened all of the cupboards and asked, "Where's the money?"

"It's under the sink," said the woman as she rushed to her husband's side. Big Ed reached under and behind the kitchen sink and pulled a large duffel bag out, heavy, full of money.

"Here's the feria," said Big Ed as he put the straps of the bag over his shoulder.

"Orale, let's get going," I said. Then I pointed my rifle to the couple, "If you ever tell anyone about this, I'll chop you up into pieces!"

The woman was no longer talking back; she was full of fear. I followed Big Ed out of the house and quickly walked back towards the ranfla. I drove straight to the freeway, not wanting this much cash in my house. I dialed my tió s phone number on my cellular.

"Hello," I said.

"Hola, mijo. ¿Qué pasa?" he asked.

"I need to go and take you something, right now," I said.

"Ok, I'll wait up for you," said my tió.

"I'll be there in an hour or so. I'm with Big Ed," I said as I hung the phone up.

I put the phone down and thought of everything that had happened. I was to the point that I didn't care anymore, selling and transporting drugs, violence, murder. It didn't matter. I'm not saying that I was a cold blooded man. I had just learned to handle my business. I couldn't be weak in this type of lifestyle. I loved Angelina, I loved my parents and I loved my tió and homeboys. But a man couldn't let the compassion he had for his loved ones get in the way of doing what he had to do. I had to learn to separate any feelings of sorrow or mercy from the business or my organization.

Don Chavelin Sanchez was only expecting the man to be killed, not expecting his money to be returned. Because Big Ed helped me, I wanted to give him some of the feria. I was sure Don Chavelin wouldn't mind. As for me, I just wanted to quit selling. And by me doing this one last thing for him, I was hoping that I wouldn't have problems. I was bringing in a lot of feria for my tió and Don Chavelin. I wanted to hand everything down to Big Ed, that is if he wanted to take over. It would be a smooth transaction.

We finally arrived to my tió's and were now sitting in the living room with him.

"Did you take care of our problem?" asked my tió.

"Yeah... he's dead," I said.

"Good, good. Don Chavelin will be happy to hear the news," said my tió.

"Well, the reason I came down here is to hide the guns we used. Can you have someone hide them for me?" I said.

"Si, claro. I'll call someone right now to come to get them," said my tió.

"I also wanted to talk to you about something else," I said.

"Is something else wrong?" he asked concerned.

"Angelina is almost due... she has about two more weeks to go. Remember when you told me to sell until I made enough money, then open a legit business? Well, I'm ready to quit... I want to be legal," I said. "I not only got rid of Don Chavelins problem, I brought some of his money back. And by giving Don Chavelin his money, and for getting rid of Lencho, I was hoping Don Chavelin wouldn't have a problem with me quitting. I want to hand the business over to Big Ed," I said.

"What? You got some of his money back?" asked my tió surprised.

"Yeah, I got a spare tire and a duffel bag full of money. I don't know how much is in there. I want to give Big Ed some for helping me, then I'll leave it all to you. I'll let you give it back to him," I said.

"Well, mijo. You did it! You did a good job!" said my tió as he stood up, laughed and walked over to hug me. "Of course you can quit. I'm really proud of you mijo."

"Really tió, proud?" I asked.

"Yes, of course! I knew you had my blood pumping through your heart," he said. "I'm going to call Don Chavelin to let him know the good news," said my tió as he lifted the phone and dialed. He waited for a few seconds then said, "Hola, Don Chavelin. Soy Cuerno de California."

"That problem is taken care of... Yes... I also want you to know something else.... He got some of the money back for you," said my tió.

I was wondering what Don Chavelin was saying on the other side of the line. My uncle talked for a minute or so longer, then handed the phone over to me. I took it and said, "Hola, Don Chavelin."

"¿Cómo estas?" asked Don Chavelin.

"I'm doing good, really good," I answered feeling nervous.

"So you got some of my money back?" he asked.

"Yes, I'm going to give some to my camarada that helped me tonight. Then I'm going to leave the rest here with my tió, for you," I said.

"You are an honest man Joaquín. I didn't ask you to get me the money... you could have kept all of it," he said.

"I would never do that to you Don Chavelin. I see you in the highest respect," I said.

"...Good, if more men were like you, these things wouldn't happen. I want to thank you... personally. I can't have the money sent to me by mail. You can't bring that much cash on a plane, so someone needs to drive it down. I want you and your tió to drive down here. I'll pay for everything. Come and have a vacation at my expense," said Don Chavelin. "You can stay in my guest house I have next to my home in el rancho."

"Thank you, Don Chavelfn. We'll leave tonight," I said. I hadn't planned on this happening.

"Have you ever been to Mexico?" asked Don Chavelin.

"No, but I've always wanted to go. My father taught me about the history... I would like to go to Mexico City." I paused as I remembered my baby and Angelina. "There's a problem though... my girlfriend is pregnant, and she's due in two weeks. How long would my stay be?" I asked.

"Oh... if you can't come I'll understand. Even though I must admit I was hoping to thank you in person. I'm sure you could come for only three or four days, the choice is yours. I'm not forcing you," said the Don understandably.

"No, I'll go. Four days away from home is fine. I'll be seeing you," I said hanging the phone up.

After I hung up I told my tió about the trip. He had my tia Isabel pack our bags, since I still had clothes in the room when I stayed. We took the duffel bag and spare tire out of my trunk and counted it in the garage. We had the money laid out on the floor on a blanket. Big Ed, my tió and I all counted separate piles. When we finished it totaled to seven hundred thousand dollars in hundreds, fifties, twenties and tens. I counted out a hundred thousand dollars and handed it to Big Ed, "This is for you carnal. You've always been there for me, bro."

"Damn homie, are you sure? That's a lot of feria to hand someone," said Big Ed hesitating to take the money.

"Just take it," I said. Take my car back and leave it at Angelinas. I'll call her and tell her that your going to drop it off. I'll be back in a few days."

"Do you want me to go with you carnal?" said, Big Ed.

"Don Chavelin only wants my tió and me to go," I said.

"Si, Don Chavelin is very strict as to who goes into his home. Don't worry about Joaquín, I'll take care of him," said my tió to Big Ed.

We all shook hands, then I handed Big Ed my keys. Then we got into my tió's Mercedes and drove southbound toward Mexico. I didn't know what to expect in Mexico. While on the freeway I called Angelina from my cellular phone.

"Hello? It's me, Joaquín," I said to Angelina as soon as she answered.

"Where are you? Are you ok?" she said worried.

"Don't worry, baby. I'm gonna be gone for a few days," I said.

"What! I thought you said that you were finished!" said Angelina.

"I can't explain right now, mija. I am done, but I need to finish what I started. I promise it's going to be ok."

"I don't have a good feeling about this. Please just come home. Baby, I need you here with me... please just come home," begged Angelina. I could hear her begin to cry.

"Don't do that! I'll be gone no more than four days, I need to do this. I'm sorry, but I'm gonna get off the phone now," I said.

"I love you, Joaquín," said Angelina.

"I love you también... don't worry, ok," I said as we hung up. I hesitated to hang the phone up. It felt as if she was far away, but I knew thatsoon I would be with her.

I sat quietly, then my tió asked, "Are you ok, mijo?"

"Yeah, I'm ok," I answered.

"Listen mijo, if you want to go back, I'll take you back. It's ok, I can explain to Don Chavelin," offered my tió.

"No. Don't worry about me. Let's just go and do this," I said. My tió didn't bring it up again. He knew that I was determined to deliver the money to Don Chavelin. It was hours before we reached the Mexican border. We had driven all night. Somehow I felt as if my life would change with this trip. Mexico was going to change my life.

14

As we passed the Mexican border my tió explained some facts to me.

"Look, this is nothing like back home. It's a whole new different onda. We are going to drive down this interstate that goes through most of Mexico. There are toll booths throughout the freeway. If we get questioned about where we are heading, tell them that there is a death in the family, and that we are going to a funeral in Michoacin. If the federales decide to search the vehicle, make sure you watch them every second. They are known to plant a bag of cocaine on cars. That way they can blackmail and keep the ranfla."

I just sat and listened as I stared at the landscape. I had heard so much of Mexico while growing up, yet it was different seeing it. All I had were stories, but here I was, in the same land that Pancho Villa rode through. How it must of looked with General Villa riding on his horse, rifle in hand. I smiled to myself as I thought of my father. I liked being here with my tió, but I would have enjoyed it if my father was here with me. I could hear his voice telling me of my great grandfather. Those times must have been hypnotizing, fighting with sweat and blood for your land. Now everything was spoils of war. There was nothing worth fighting for. Either you had money or you didn't. Emiliano Zapata and Pancho Villa would of been ashamed of how Mexicano's lived. To think that they fought and died so our raza could kill each other for neighborhoods. Most Mexican's were still not educated, were still in the fields and factories, and still lived in the poorest neighborhoods. If the only way for me to rise out of poverty was to sell drugs, then I was determined to sell the most.

Halfway to Michoacán, we stopped at a small motel and slept. We had been taking turns driving, but we were exhausted. We ate at a small restaurant that had the best enchiladas I had ever tasted. With sleep and food in our stomachs, we continued our drive. We were now only a few hours away from Michoacin. Mountains were everywhere as we drove toward the rancho; it looked beautiful. We were in the Sierra, where the toughest Méxicano's come from. This was where most of the marijuana, chiva and crank was transported from to the United States. Everything from drug dealers, drug runners, bandits and murderers hid in these mountains.

As we reached el rancho I sat up in my seat. I saw the biggest house I had ever seen. Huge trees and perfectly cut green grass looked like a painted picture as it rolled across acres and acres of land. We stopped at a huge gated entrance leading toward the house. Two men stood there, and waved us in. They must of been expecting us. I could tell they were carrying guns and with eyes of hawks. We slowly drove towards the large white house as Don Chavelfn walked out to greet us.

"Hola, welcome to my home," said Don Chavelfn as he shook our hands and hugged us. "How is my daughter?"

"She is doing good... she said that she misses you," answered my tió.

"Yes... yes. I miss her every single day. Not a day goes by that I don't pray for her to be happy," said Don Chavelfn.

"Next time, I will bring her," said my tió.

"That would be nice," said Don Chavelfn. Then he looked toward me and asked, "So how do you like Mexico?"

"It's a beautiful country, sefior. Maybe someday I can own a house with landscape like yours," I said.

"I'm sure you will someday. Come on inside, I know your hungry," said Don Chavelfn as he turned and walked toward his house. My tió opened the trunk and we pulled our bags out, including the bag full of money. The house was full of large portraits. It seemed as if each portrait portrayed a part of Mexican History. One portrait in particular caught my eye; it was of Pancho Villa and Emiliano Zapata meeting for the first time.

"Do you like that painting?" asked Don Chavelfn.

"Yes, my father told me stories about the Revolution of 1910. These were great men," I answered.

"Si, lo fueron. They were brave men, men that fought for the people," said Don Chavelfn. "This portrait is of a picture taken when they met in Mexico City. This was a great moment for our people."

I admired the portrait as Don Chavelfn talked to my tió. Before I went back home, I needed to go to Mexico City. I wanted to see and feel the same ground these great revolutionaries walked on. I wanted to see the old buildings, mix with the people and see pyramids of the Aztecs. Then it occurred to me that I could buy a camcorder and record all of it for Angelina. That way she could see the things I would see.

We all sat in his living room as I opened the duffel bag of money. I pulled out stack after stack, covering the entire coffee table.

"I've brought you six hundred thousand dollars. I originally had seven hundred thousand but I paid my good camarada for his time in helping me. I hope that you don't mind," I said.

"No, of course I don't mind. This is money I wasn't expecting," said Don Chavelfn as he stared at the money then back at me. "How can I repay you?"

"You can repay me by letting me live a legal life with my girlfriend. I know you don't force me or anyone to sell, but I want you to approve. I still want to be respected by you," I answered.

"Yes, go and live a good life. Not many men your age have accomplished what you have. You've shown me that you are willing to make money, you've shown your loyalty to me by returning this money, and you've murdered for me. Lencho was a no good thief." He paused then asked, "Tell me... how did he die?" asked Don Chavelfn.

I looked around, feeling uncomfortable. I looked at my tió as he nodded his head, sort of like a green light to tell Don Chavelfn the story.

"I took him out to the country, shot him in each leg as he begged for his life. Then I let him know that this was for Don Chavelfn. Then I unloaded an entire thirty round clip into his chest. Once I finished I put him in the trunk of his car and pushed it into an aqueduct," I said.

"Ha, hahaha. I love to hear stories like that," said Don Chavelfn.

I nodded in agreement, knowing Don Chavelfn was the most

brutal man I had ever known. He practically owned the nearby town. No one would ever think of crossing him. He wouldn't just kill you, he would torture your family in front of you, then kill you.

Later that evening Don Chavelfn and I drove into town in his new Bronco. My tió stayed at the house to get some rest. Most of the people in the small town looked poor. He carried a huge forty five semi-automatic gun where ever he went. We drove to the only place that carried camcorders. I bought one and a bag of video tapes. Everytime we drove by a police officer, they would wave at Don Chavelfn.

"Can I ask you a question?" I asked Don Chavelín.

"Sure, ask me anything you want," he said.

"Do the police know what you do for a living? I notice that they all wave to you."

He laughed saying, "That's a good quesTión. Of course they know what I do. They would never dare try to arrest me... I paid for their new police department," said Don Chavelfn.

"I don't understand... I hate cops," I said.

"Things are different here. Traficantes run this place. The police know who they can push around and who they can't. If they ever tried to give me problems, I would simply have their familia's killed. It would be nothing to take an officer to the mountains and put a bullet in their head, or to kill him in broad daylight at the plaza downtown. In Mexico, the most vicious is the one that controls. For instance, if you moved down here and tried growing and transporting marijuana without me, the police would have every right to take you down, and you wouldn't be able to do anything about it. But if you moved down here and worked for me, no one could touch you. You could drive around in a new Lexus, wearing diamonds and gold, carrying a cuerno de chivo, and if they stopped you, the only words you would say is, 'Trabajo por Don Chavelfn Sanchez'. Don't get me wrong, sometimes men try to rob me. Like Lencho, but people like that never last."

I listened as we drove through town. In the middle of all the poverty, new trucks and cars drove around. It was very obvious. I couldn't believe the fact that men sold drugs openly here, with the protection of Don Chavelfn.

"The only men I have to worry about is the federales. They don't come from the police department, but from the Mexican army. And believe me, when they come to surround the house, they don't have intentions of arresting you. So the best thing you can do is get your biggest and fastest machine gun and have it out with them, because no matter what your not going to make it out alive. Like Emiliano Zapata said, it's better to die on your feet than to live on your knees, no?" explained Don Chavelfn.

We drove back to the house and walked in. My tió had just woken up and was going to take a shower. We were invited to stay in the guest home that had three bedrooms. I grabbed my bag of clothes and took them to the guest house. I ironed and took a long cool shower. Don Chavelfn took us to his favorite restaurant for dinner.

"So what are you men going to be doing while in Mexico?" asked Don Chavelfn as we waited for our plates.

"I don't know," said my tió.

"I want to go see Mexico City," I said.

"When and how are you going? It is a beautiful city, full of culture," said Don Chavelfn.

"I wanted to drive there tomorrow," I answered.

"Nonsense, I'll get you a plane ticket for the morning flight out. When you are here with me, you go first class," said Don

Chavelfn.

"Are you sure?" I asked.

"Of course I'm sure. I'll have the ticket set up for you by tonight," answered Don Chavelfn.

"Gracias, I would appreciate that," I said.

Our dinners were served by the restaurant owner himself. Don Chavelfn Sanchez thanked him, and we began to eat. We talked about everything, money, land and the future. I thought back to the time the homeboys and I would sit at the park, waiting for trouble. My future back then was focused on being in control of my neighborhood and the war on VSL Now, here, I was with one of the most feared men in Michoacin, eating dinner with him. When we got back to the house, Don Chavelfn reserved a round trip flight for me at seven thirty in the morning. He also reserved a suite at the Marquís Hotel. My tió didn't want to go, saying he had some other business to take care of. I was tired and sleepy so I went to the guest house to get rest. I set the clock and fell asleep.

I never thought I would be in Mexico, much less on a plane, first class. The view from the small window was unbelievable as we passed over mountains and valleys. I thought of my father. He would have loved to be here with me. I've wanted to see Mexico City ever since I could remember. I knew that I was going to learn a lot about my Raza by seeing the pyramids and museum.

I looked out of the window as the plane was ready to land. The city extended as far as the eye could see. I knew that Mexico City was big, but I didn't realize just how big it really was. Before the plane landed I pulled out the video camera and recorded the city from the sky. I was here for one night, so I wanted to get the most out of it. I only had luggage for one day, and I carried it on the plane. I walked out to the front of the airport and took a taxi to the hotel. The airport was just over a half hour to my destination. The streets were full of people and cars. I was going to stay at the Hotel

Marquís Reforma, one mile from Chapultepec Park. The park was where the city zoo was located. It was the most wooded area in all of the city. It was also one of the many sites of the battle between the Spaniards and Aztecs.

As I walked inside the hotel, the lobby was luxurious with huge chandeliers hanging. The entire lobby was luxurious. Most of the guests were white. It was amusing to me, being that I was in Mexico. Even though I'd been making a lot of feria, I still dressed like a cholo. It was the style I chose to wear. Here I was, standing in a lobby full of White tourists with gray Ben Davis pants creased and a white t-shirt. I walked up to the reception desk to get my room key. They already had my reservation in the computer system. They thanked me for choosing the Marquis Reforma Hotel then I was told what floor my room was in. I took the elevator to the fifteenth floor then walked down a hall to my room. As I walked in I instantly knew I was staying in a luxury hotel because it looked more like an apartment than a hotel room, complete with mini bar, hot tub, fax machine, and sofas. I walked to the window and looked out to see the view. I was in awe. I videotaped the old palace in Chapultepec Park that could easily be seen from my room. I didn't want to waste my time in the room so I put my bags away and walked downstairs.

The first thing I did was walk over to Chapultepec Park. I bought a drink from a small vendor as I sat in the shade recording all of the gente passing by. Families walked by with their kids smiling and laughing. I knew that someday I would be here again with Angelina and my child.

I had no idea where the Aztec pyramids were, and I didn't know where anything was at. But here I was in one of the biggest cities in the world. I waved a taxi down and told him

I wanted to go to the nearest Aztec pyramid.

"O, ¿quiéres ir al Templo Mayor," said the taxi driver.

"Si, por favor," I answered.

"Ok," said the driver.

We drove downtown as I looked out of the window. We passed large buildings with beautiful murals. The taxi stopped in front of a museum, "Here it is," said the man in broken English.

"Gracias," I said as I paid him and stepped out.

Then I walked to the museum and paid admission. The Templo Mayor was the most important temple to the Aztecs, but it was buried by the Spaniards. Most of it was still underground. Inside were hundreds of Aztec artifacts, even the Aztec calendar. It was huge as I looked down at it. When the Spaniards invaded Mexico and defeated the Aztecs, they tried to hide the history. Books were destroyed, temples were torn down, and churches were built on top of Aztec structures. The Aztec calendar was buried because it was too massive to break and destroy.

Being in Mexico City made me think of Zapata and Villa meeting for the first time, two Mexican men not ashamed of their indigenous heritage. I could imagine Pancho Villa on his horse, plodding along in the downtown streets of the city, laughing as he took the photograph sitting in the presidents chair alongside Emiliano Zapata. The two greatest men of Mexico, demanding the rich bow down. They eventually would.

As I walked through the museum and read about the history of my culture, it seemed to come alive. For years I had never given thought to my history, caring only about Barrio Apache. As I saw these ancient artifacts, they seemed to pull and tug at my soul. If I would have been alive during the invasion of Mexico by the Spaniards, I would have fought to the death along with the Aztecs, or even during the Mexican Revolution of 1910. But instead, I was dealing drugs to people that probably didn't even know their history or much less care. What a shame that for centuries Mexicans had fought for freedom and land, and now most of the Raza in the United States was either dead, slanging dope, addicted, or in the pinta. Seeing these artifacts gave me a feeling of confusion within myself. I should have known better than to gangbang or deal dope. I knew my history and I embraced it, but I also knew that either you sold dope or you lived in low-income housing clutching at every dollar.

After a few hours, I walked back to the front of the museum. I didn't want to spend my entire day inside there. My stomach growled as I realized that I hadn't eaten breakfast.

I walked out and waved a taxi down. As I got in, the man asked me where I wanted to go. I told him to drive to a good restaurant.

"Ok, I know a good restaurant just down the street," said the man.

"Good, cause I'm starving," I replied.

We drove a few blocks and came upon a huge block square in the middle of the city. There were thousands of people yelling, and it looked like a rally. On one side of the square was an old tall church, and on the other stood a government building.

"Let me out here," I said to the driver. I paid him and stepped out. People were holding large banners that had a mans face on it, covered by a ski mask. Others had banners of Emiliano Zapata with the words, 'Tierra y Libertad'. I thought to myself, 'What the hell is all this about?' I saw others with signs that read, 'Zapatista, EZLN'. These people were in such a rage that it shocked me. Some of the gente were yelling with their fists up in the air, as they wore panos or ski masks to cover their face. I walked around trying to figure out what was going on.

"¿Quiéres comprar una camiseta?" asked an older man holding t-shirts and stickers.

"No se," I said as I looked at a t-shirt. It had a drawing of a man with a ski mask and the words ¡No mas! written on it.

"¿Quién es?" I asked the man as I pointed to the shirt.

"Es Subcomandante Marcos," answered the man.

"Well, I don't know who that is," I said.

"¿No sabes? ¿Eres Mexicano? Ah, eres un pocho," said the man.

"Soy Mexicano de Califas!" I answered feeling disrespected.

"Ja, ja, ja, don't get mad about it," said the man. "I'm only joking around with you, hombre. Me llamo Nicolas."

"Orale pues, me llamo Joaquin," I said as we shook hands.

"Nice to meet you Joaquín," said Nicolas.

"Are you going to tell me who this is on this t-shirt?" I asked.

"It's me, it's you, it's everyone here," answered Nicolds.

"What are you talking about?"

"It is Subcomandante Marcos, speaker for the Zapatista army of Chiapas."

"¿Qué? What do you mean Zapatistas? The revolution ended decades ago. Why are all of these gentes out here for?" I asked.

"You got it all wrong. Zapata is alive, his horse still rides through the mountains," said Nicolds with his eyes closed, as if in a trance. "The Zapatista army rose once again for land, so Zapata still lives through us, the indigenous people."

"I have no idea of what you are talking about," I said shaking my head and looking around at the demonstrators.

"Do you really want to know? I can see the sincerity in your eyes. Your searching for something, aren't you?" said Nicolds.

"I'm just here on vacation," I snapped quickly, calm, knowing he was right.

"No, you're wrong. Destiny has brought you here," said Nicolás.

For the first time, I looked at this man. Something about him seemed wise and truthful. He was small and thin. He looked like he was in his fifties. He wore sandals and a long sleeved shirt that was worn thin. His eyes looked old and worn, eyelids down low almost completely covering his deep carved eyes. He looked weak and brittle compared to myself. I laughed at the thought that this man saw himself as a Zapatista. I had always imagined Zapata and his men as big men with bullets across their chest on a horse, fighting, with big mustaches and yelling gritos of victory.

"Ok, tell me more," I asked out of curiosity.

"I will tell anyone that is interested in the uprising of our people," said Nicolds.

"The Zapatista Army, the EZLN rose up in arms to fight for their land. For years we have worked only to make the government rich. My people in the state of Chiapas have nothing, no food, clothes or medicine. We had no choice but to fight with sticks, rocks and broken guns. We would train high up in the mountains, just waiting for the perfect time to attack. We saved every bullet we had, collected as many guns as possible."

"Are you serious? Why didn't I know about any of this?" I asked amazed. I wondered why my father hadn't mentioned any of this to me. Or maybe I just wasn't listening.

"You need to open your eyes. You worry about how many

cars you have, or how much gold you have. While we are here trying to survive another day. On new year's eve, in 1994 we took over San Cristobal de las Casas, Chiapas. We did it as a statement to show the world the injustices that we suffered in Mexico. And what did the Mexican government do? They sent military tanks and helicopters given to them by the United States, and they came into our villages and shot women, children, and men." Nicolás paused for a few seconds as the corner of his eye quivered and a small tear rolled down his brown cheek. "They shot my wife and two grandkids, then they raped my daughter and butchered her husband. I begged for them to kill me..."

I didn't know what to say to this man. His tears now rolled down his old wrinkled face. He wiped his eyes and looked directly at me, "I have nothing left... I have no home, I have no peace, no wife and no family. They have taken it all from me."

"I'm sorry, I didn't realize this was going on," I said seeing the pain in his eyes. Was this true? How could things like this happen this day and age? I asked, "So what is happening now? Why are all of these people here?"

"We are continually being slaughtered in Chiapas by the military, paramilitaries, and ranchers. Men are taken from their homes and executed, and our women are raped and dumped along dirt roads... pregnant women's bellies sliced open, and babies killed in front of their mother. Then they're left alive to die slowly. What kind of government would allow such a thing? We are here to make a statement. We've rebelled in Chiapas, but soon all of Mexico will rebel!" said Nicolás standing straight. He no longer looked like an old brittle man. "We are the faceless warriors. We are Zapatistas!"

It felt as if every single story my father had taught me suddenly came alive. The revolution of 1910 wasn't a part of the past, but here, in this place. All of these years I felt as if the people no longer cared as if it were every man for himself. But here people were once again proud, strong, my Raza, rallying for a cause more important than a barrio or drug deals. This old man wasn't impressed by my money or power. He wanted justice like Emiliano Zapata wanted justice.

"Why are people wearing ski masks or panos to cover their face?" I asked.

"If we show our faces to the military, our families and friends will be tortured and killed. By covering our faces we make a statement. We are a faceless army. We do not want fame or medals or personal glory. We are all Zapata, and we are all Zapatistas and we are all Subcomandante Marcos. I will die before I choose to give up this fight. I will fight knowing that my blood was spilled for my indigenous people. Subcomandante Marcos once told me a saying, "Without struggle, there is no change." We are sick and tired of being stepped on, and I will aim and shoot anyone opposing our justice!" said Nicolds.

"How can I help?" I asked surprised by my own question. "I can help you fight, I have the means..."

"Ay, I like you Joaquín. I knew you had heart from the second I saw you. I believe you, but don't kid yourself. I also know that you are probably nicely paid. With no disrespect, I would guess that you sell drugs. You will not help us for long, because the money will drag you back into your lifestyle," said Nicolas.

"How are you going to judge me like that? You don't know anything about me! I do what I do to survive. Yes, I agree that it's a different way of survival for you, but I still survive my way. It's not easy being Mexican in the United States. My father taught me about respect and history of my Raza. He taught me about Emiliano Zapata and Pancho Villa. My own grandfather was thrown off a train during the revolution for killing a federal. The struggle runs in my veins, and I was raised to live and die for my culture!" I said.

Nicolás stood there looking around without saying a word. Then he looked right at me saying, "If your father taught you so much, why are you living this lifestyle you're living?"

"My father walked out of my life while I was in jail. I haven't talked to him in months, and I got a child coming. What the hell am I supposed to do? As a matter of fact, I'm done with that lifestyle. I'm going to put all of my money into a record company, for Raza artists."

He paused and looked at me more intensely and said, "You really want to know how to help the Zapatista struggle?" asked Nicolas.

"Of course I want to know. I'll carry any gun, and shoot any military in a second, with no hesitations," I said.

"You've got it all wrong, Joaquín," said Nicolas shaking his head. "It's not about going around killing people. We don't do it for the sake of murder. We shoot because our backs are against the wall. You need to go back home and fix things with your father, and be with your women and... you need to take your money and start your own business. But don't ever let your business and money make you forget where you came from, or forget us. We need people like you to let the Raza from the U.S. know about what's going on here."

"What are you talking about? How is that going to help?" I asked.

"First of all, familia is first. You need to have a relationship with your father. We don't need another soldier to carry a gun through the jungles! We need publicity. We need to have justice everywhere, not just in Chiapas. We as indigenous people must never give in to those that oppress us. If we live to their mold of how they want us to live, we've already lost. If you have a record company, let the music be of the struggles of our people, your people. With your music as access, you can reach thousands of more people that we can't. The only way we will win is if more of our people are educated about this struggle. We need doctors, lawyers, engineers, computer programmers, politicians, teachers, writers, musicians, and business owners to work for the struggle, to tell the world. I know that many Mexicans are educated, but once they are, they forget about us. This new Mexican revolution isn't about men on horses fighting in the thousands. It's guerrilla warfare of the mind. Warfare tactics must be fought according to the situation. In Chiapas and other states, we are forced to fight back violently. Our people in the United States has a chance to fight with their minds."

I sat and let every word sink into my mind as he continued to talk. Everything he said made perfect sense. I could release records from my label educating the Raza about Emiliano Zapata, Pancho Villa, the EZLN and Subcomandante Marcos. I could learn everything about the struggle that was happening now. It wasn't only about the Mexican Revolution of 1910, but about the revolution happening now. I felt a clearer sense of direction in my life now. I had already promised Angelina that I would stop selling drugs. But now I had a real reason to quit and start my own business. I thought to myself 'this is what being Mexicano really is' as I looked around at the people, holding up banners and closed fists. Drums played as Aztec dancers now danced in circles. Flyers were passed out with pictures of Zapatista soldiers in green camouflage, boots, ski masks, and AK-47 assault rifles.

I turned toward Nicolas, "I want to buy your shirts and stickers."

"Well, the cost is..."

"Here," I said as I put a roll of money I had in my pocket into his hand, only keeping a couple hundred.

"I can't take all of this money," said Nicolas nervous at the site of the roll of money.

"I won't take no for an answer. What you have taught me is worth more than all the money I have," I said as I only took one shirt and quickly walked away. I didn't give Nicolas a chance to catch up. I took one last look at the rally before I sat into a taxi cab.

"How are you doing sir?" asked the taxi driver.

"I'm doing good. Would you know if there are any other pyramids to see in Mexico City?" I asked.

"Oh yes, right outside of the city. You can take a bus there," said the driver.

"Gracias, can you please take me to the bus?" I asked as I sat back and looked at the scenery.

"Si, Senor."

We weren't too far from the bus station. The bus ride took roughly forty-five minutes. As the bus drove I thought about the things Nicolis had told me. I couldn't believe that these killings, rapes, and injustices were happening even after the revolution. I thought of Angelina and the baby. As soon as I got back I would show Angelina the videotape. I would tell her everything I had seen and learned. I was pretty sure that I could find good musicians and rappers for the label I was going to start, with my tió teaching me about running a record company. I knew that it would be successful, and in each release, I would make sure that at least one song or more taught Raza about what was happening in Chiapas or anywhere else. As the bus pulled up to the parking lot I could see the pyramids.

I was in awe as the biggest one named the Sun Pyramid stood aiming toward the heavens. A smaller one named Pyramid of the Moon also stood there. These ancient pyramids stood here even before the Aztecs. I held up the video camera and recorded both of the pyramids. There were also two temples and a street named Street of the Dead. The street was named that because skeletons along the path that were excavated lined the streets.

As I walked towards the Sun Pyramid, I began to walk up the steep steps. As I reached the top I imagined what a warrior felt and saw at what I saw, standing here. Tourists were all around me talking and laughing, but I closed my eyes, drowning out all sound except the wind. And imagined how it must have been in ancient times. Men dressed in battle gear, with the brightest feathers and colors, drummers playing as they danced, drums playing like a heartbeat. Huge markets filled with people buying and selling food, clothes, weapons, and animals from the farthest corners of Mexico. It must have been a time and a place where every day was a blessing, a time when the people gave thanks to the sun, the moon and the earth. How beautiful it must have been before Hernan Cortes invaded. He came with his greed and disease killing and torturing the people, burning their books and history. I could feel my blood running fast in my body as if every part of my soul knew that this was once home. My mouth wanted to cry out, 'we are still alive! The people of the Sun can never be buried and burned!'

I held out my camera and recorded the top of the pyramid for Angelina to see. Then I aimed the camera towards my face and said, "See Angelina, this is what Mexico is about." Then I walked back down the steep stairs and walked through the other temples, each time feeling more as one with the old ruins. I felt more determined than ever to make things right with my father and mother, Angelina and the baby. I had survived through unimaginable things. I had experienced things that I should not have experienced. I realized that I needed this trip to Mexico. It was something all of my Raza needed.

Before I left I sat before the Sun Pyramid and pulled out a pen and paper. I felt inspired to write something. I had never sat down to write a note, much less a letter or anything. But I felt the need to put my thoughts on paper. It was a way for me to hold on to the feelings I felt at this very moment. I wrote on the top of the paper 'Midst of My Confusion.' I looked at the pyramid and began to write. I thought of what my father had taught me when I was younger. I thought of Vince, Barrio Apache, my tio, drugs, money, homies, and Angelina. Things poured out onto the paper as I wrote with all the feelings and confusions I felt. I had known so much of the struggles and history of my culture, but I still chose to join a gang. I should have known better, but the lifestyle consumed me. Before I realized it, I was in too deep. There was no turning back, especially after Vince was killed.

I wrote and wrote, my hand moving uncontrollably. Then, my hand stopped. I finished writing and folded the paper to put it inside my pocket. The bus was ready to leave so I slowly walked toward the parking lot. I walked in and picked a window seat.

I looked back toward the pyramids and whispered 'thank you'. I saw silhouettes of Aztecs in battle gear, standing at the top of the pyramid, dancing in slow motion, preparing for battle. And at the foot of the Sun Pyramid stood Zapata on his horse, looking towards me and nodded his head. I looked around to the other people on the bus. They didn't seem to notice. I looked back and saw the Aztec dancers float down toward Zapata and their spirits became one. He rode off with a grito of 'Libertad!' As Nicolas said, Zapata still rides, not resting until liberty and justice are given to the people.

As the bus drove back towards the city, I anticipated being back home. The bus arrived at the station and I got a taxi back to the Hotel. It had been a long day, a day more important than any day I remembered. I took advantage of the first classroom service because I was too exhausted to go out for dinner. I took a good cool shower and relaxed. It was now night time and I'd depart in the morning. Before I closed my eyes to sleep, I decided to call Angelina. I picked up the phone and dialed the apartment. I heard the phone ring two times, "Hello," I heard Angelina's voice say.

"Hey, mija. It's me," I said.

"Joaquín! I was just thinking about you. Are you ok? How is it over there?" asked Angelina.

"Mexico is beautiful. I'm doing ok, besides that fact that I miss you. After the baby is born I want us to come for a week or two. I know you'll like it," I said.

"I would like that. I think it would be fun to be there with you," said Angelina.

"Simón, its kind of lonely without you." I paused then said, "I've learned so much today, I can't wait to tell you when I get back home and show you everything..."

"Huh, things you've learned? What do you mean?"

"I'll explain it all to you when I get home. The reason I called is that I wanted to hear your voice. I know that I've dragged you through a lot of stress, but it's all going to change. I just wanted you to know that you mean everything to me... you always have. I knew that you were the one for me the day I met you. I love everything about you... your eyes, your lips, your mind, your body, and your love."

Angelina didn't say a thing on the other line.

"Are you there?" I asked.

"Yes... I'm here. You don't know how long I've waited for you to say those words to me. I know that you love me, Joaquín. But I just needed to hear it. I'm going to love you forever, for as long as I live. Just hurry up and come home, baby!" laughed Angelina.

"Ok, mija, I'll hurry home," I said feeling good from hearing her voice.

"Bye," she said, "I'll see you when you get home."

"Ok, bye. I love you, con todo mi corazon," I said as I hung up the phone. I felt totally at ease as I closed my eyes and fell asleep.

I dreamed again of Angelina in labor at the hospital. We were excited as she pushed for the baby to come out. The doctor was coaching her to keep pushing. I felt happy as I held her hand. But the doctor was no longer Juan de Culiacan with his silent screams; it was her regular doctor. She gave one more push and I heard a baby cry. It was the most exciting thing I ever heard. I kissed Angelina on her forehead as the doctor said, "congratulations! You have a baby..." then I woke up.

I turned off the alarm and quickly took a shower, ironed, got dressed and packed. My plane was leaving in two hours. Then I took the elevator to the lobby and checked out. I walked out and took a taxi to the airport. In the gift shop, I bought a few postcards for Angelina.

The flight back to Michoacan was fast. Once I arrived I walked out to the front of the airport. My tio and Don

Chavelin Sanchez were both there waiting for me.

"Hey, mijo," said my tio as he hugged me.

"How did you like it?" asked Don Chavelin.

"This is a beautiful country. I wish I could stay longer," I said.

"Well, once the baby is born you are welcome to come back and stay in my house," said Don Chavelin.

"Gracias," I answered.

"When did you want to leave, Joaquín? We can leave now or tonight, whichever you prefer," said my tio.

"I would like to leave now. I really need to get back. Angelina's home by herself and she's almost due," I said.

"Ok, we can leave as soon as we get back to Don Chavelín's house."

As soon as we got back to Don Chavelin's house my tio and I packed all of our bags. We put them all into the trunk as Don Chavelin walked out and said, "Joaquín, I want to talk to you before you go."

"Of course," I said as I walked toward him.

"You risked a lot for me for getting rid of my problem in your town. You didn't have to bring me the money you did. Like I said before, you could have lied to me and kept it. I would have never known, and for that I am grateful... here, this is for you," he said as he handed me a thick envelope.

"You don't have to do this," I said.

"Don't argue, I won't hear it. There are a hundred thousand dollars in there. Keep it as a gift for the baby coming, and may God bless you and your familia," said Don Chavelin as he held his hand out to shake. We shook hands then hugged. Then my tió hugged him and we were off.

The drive back felt faster than when we were coming. I explained to my tio everything I had seen and learned. He never argued or talked against any of it. I told him of Nicolds and of the rally. I told him of the pyramids and the temples. He agreed to everything I was telling him, but deep down inside I knew he would never change, and I didn't expect him too. He was who he was, and nothing was going to change that.

We drove all day and late into the night before we stopped to get a room for some rest. We needed to get a few hours of sleep before we got back on the road. I just wanted to be back home in my own bed. After sleeping for six hours we took showers, ate breakfast in a small restaurant and drove off again. We had no problems getting across the border. I had the money stashed in my pants, even though we didn't have clavo. I didn't trust the judiciales, border patrol or anyone else. I felt closer to home as we passed the state line into California. I knew that I was only a few hours away from home. We drove up highway five all the way back to my tio's house, taking turns driving and letting each other sleep. We were exhausted as we finally pulled up to his driveway. Isabel came running out.

"Cuerno!"

"Hi," said my tio as they hugged. Then she came to me and hugged me as well.

"Come in," she said to us as my tió unloaded his bags. I also took my bag out to put in my car when I realized that Big Ed had taken my ranfla.

"How am I going to get home? Big Ed took my ranfla back to my house," I said.

"You take my car, just bring it back tomorrow," said my tio in a good mood.

"Orale," I said as he handed me his keys. I put my bag in the back seat and sat down to drive home.

Saying goodbye to my tio and tia, I drove off toward the

freeway, trying to hurry back home. I put a CD on of Los 4 Grandes del Norte. They were my favorite Narco-corrido group. I put the volume up and let the windows down. At two in the morning, the air smelled fresh.

16

———————

As I pulled off the freeway in town I realized the gas gauge read empty and I needed gas. The closest gas station still open was on the main street, where Barrio Apache ended. I didn't have a cuete on me but them chavalas from VSL were never around anyway. I pulled up to the gas pump and got out of the ranfla. I pulled out a twenty dollar bill so I could take to the cashier.

I walked into the store and said, "I'll put twenty dollars on pump five," to the teller who was reading a newspaper.

Then I walked out to the car and pumped the gas. I felt hungry so I decided to grab a burger at the twenty-four-hour burger stand close by. People were always there, truckers, gente working graveyard, people traveling and driving through the town. The parking lot was always full no matter what time. They had the best burgers in town. I finished gassing up and headed to the burger place. I parked in the farthest corner and walked in.

As I stood in line I noticed a lowrider full of cholos pull up into the parking lot, I didn't recognize the ranfla. I could see them looking in as I ordered. 'Damn I thought to myself for not having a cuete or filero. I sat down to wait for my order. I held my breath hoping they weren't enemies of mine. I wasn't no punk, but this was just the wrong time. I just wanted to get my food and go home. I could see them from the corner of my eye as they stepped out of the ranfla. I looked straight ahead as they walked in. I counted four of them. I held my breath as I felt my heart jumping. It seemed as if no one noticed the tension as they kept eating. Men, women, and children were laughing and talking. The cholos seemed to stand there for hours. I could tell that they were staring right at me. I could see one of them walk towards me.

"Remember me, ese," said the Cholo.

I turned to look at him, I didn't recognize his face. He had his head shaved with a mustache and goatee, a tear tattooed below the side of his eye.

"Chale, I don't know you, vato," I said.

"Well maybe you'll remember me by this," he said as he lifted his shirt and showed me a scar from a bullet wound in his chest. I looked at his face again and I recognized him as the vato I had shot at the park.

"I've waited for a long time to catch up to you, ese," said the cholo.

I stood up and faced him, "This isn't the time and day for this. That was a long time ago," I said.

"Damn right that was a long time ago! I only breath with one lung!" he said. Then he took a swing as I ducked. It all seemed to go slow moTión as we fought. I could hear everyone panic as we threw blow after blow at each other. The other cholos ran towards me and began punching me. I hit one of them solid on his jaw as he fell. The vato I had shot began yelling "Varrio Side Locos rifamos!" Then he pulled out a cuete as I fought him and his homeboys. He let a shot out, and it hit a window. I managed to punch him right under his ribs, making him lose all air. His body went weak as I reached for his gun. I felt kicks and punches all over my body.

Their yells no longer made sense to me. It all sounded drowned and distorted. In the middle of the commotion, they didn't realize I now had the cuete. I aimed at the cholo in front of me, and I pulled the trigger. In an instant, his face exploded and his body went limp and fell. The other cholos stopped punching and kicking as I aimed at another cholo, and I pulled the trigger and shot him. He fell and began twitching with blood gushing out of his mouth. A cholo that had been outside came running in screaming at the top of his lungs, "Puro VSL! You're going to die!"

I shot at him and missed. He also aimed and began shooting at me. 'Women were screaming and crying. The vato I had taken the gun from tried to stand up as I shot him in the head, sending him falling face forward like a rag doll. One of the other cholos ran out of the building followed by the cholo with the gun. People were laying down as I ran out trying to get to my ranfla. The cholo came running back and shooting at me as I shot at him. I felt something burning in my gut, and looking down I saw blood. I pulled the trigger one last time and hit a cholo on his leg. He fell and began screaming in pain. I ran toward my car as he continued shooting at me. The bullets flew by me. I got in my car and headed toward the country. 'What am I going to do?' I said to myself. I couldn't go home, and I couldn't go to my parents or Big Ed's. The cops were going to be looking for me. I just killed two men. "Damn it!" I screamed at the top of my lungs as I drove farther away from town, farther away from home. The burning from the bullet wound was getting worse. I was losing a lot of blood. I followed a small road to an old abandoned barn. I remembered that I had my video camera with me. I reached into my bag sitting in the back seat and made sure it was still there. I had to let Angelina know what happened.

"And here I am now, telling my story to this camera. I know what is going to happen... I feel weaker as each minute passes. It's ok though, I've accepted my fate a long time ago. I told this story for you Angelina, and my mother and father and for my unborn baby. I wanted you to know that I really wanted to change. I really wanted to make a difference. I'm sure the police are at your houses right now as I record this. I didn't mean for any of it to happen. Don't believe everything the cops tell you. I'm a man that had dreams. I... wanted to live a good decent life. It just seemed that my life was full of distortion and clouds, clouds that stopped me from seeing things clearly. The more I tried to change the worse things got. And to my unborn baby, I want to tell you that I love you. I loved your mother with all of my heart. Use this story to make your life better... your mother deserves a good life.

And to my mother and father. Please forgive me for everything I dragged you through. I didn't mean it, I was just lost. I was looking for something, but I didn't know what. Dad, remember when you told me you were ashamed of me when I was in jail. I don't think you realize how much it hurt me. All my life I just wanted your approval. You are everything to me. I never did forget all the stories you told me. I wanted so much to be the man you wanted me to be. I just wanted you to be proud of me."

Then the tape ended and the recorder stopped.

17

Angelina waited all night for Joaquín to show up. As she laid in bed she could hear gunshots in the distance. She felt a cold chill throughout her body. "Please God, please let Joaquín get home safely," she prayed as tears ran down her face.

The next morning Joaquín was found dead by an old Mexican farmer. Everyone in town was talking about the shoot-out in the burger stand. Angelina found out about Joaquín when the police knocked on her door looking for Joaquín. They told her that he was wanted for murder. She was told that he killed two other men in cold blood and shot another. She fell back on her couch as they questioned her.

News about Joaquín's body being found spread fast as detectives and the coroner went to the old abandoned barn. Angelina went into a panic, locking herself in her room. She couldn't believe he was gone. She felt as if her heart and soul were gone. How could he be gone, she thought. The tears wouldn't stop as she felt the baby kick, the baby Joaquín would never hold in his arms. The baby would never hear his voice or hear his laugh. She fainted and fell on her bed, dreaming of her and Joaquín together again.

Joaquín's father went into a rage when detectives showed up to tell him his son's body was found. They had smirks on their faces as they told him that he was dead. He couldn't believe it as he kicked and punched the walls of his home. He screamed out in pain, hoping it was all a bad nightmare. "Get out!" he screamed at the detectives. He ripped at his shirt and skin, wanting to take the place of his son.

Joaquín's little brother sat in his room with his mother, tears falling to his lap. He didn't understand why his brother was gone. He had grown up wanting to be like him. His mother silently cried, her heart ached with so much pain.

Two days later an old man showed up at Joaquín's father's house.

"Hello, can I help you?" said Joaquín's father.

"Si, I came to bring this to you," said the old man.

"What is it? I don't understand."

"Are you Joaquín's father?" asked the man.

"Yes," Joaquín's father answered.

"I'm the man that found your son and called the police. He left this note for whoever found him. It said to please give this camera and envelope to his father and to not let the police get ahold of any of this. I know how the gringos are in this country, so I hid the camera before they came... I am sorry about your loss," said the man.

Joaquín's father took the envelope and camera and shook the man's hand.

"Gracias," said Joaquín's father.

"De nada," answered the man as he walked off.

As he closed the door he opened the envelope, and inside

was the most hundreds he had ever seen, along with a poem. The next day at the funeral all of Joaquín's friends and familia were around. Angelina, his mother, Father, and brother, Big Ed, Alfredo, Dragon, Spider, Tobo and countless other homeboys and homegirls from Barrio Apache. Cuerno and Isabel couldn't make it. He was being investigated to see if he had any part in the murders because Joaquín was driving his Mercedes during the shooting. His tio had thousands of dollars worth of flowers sent to the funeral home. The funeral home was filled to capacity as they all sat for the service.

After the pastor spoke his sermon he asked if anyone wanted to speak. Joaquín's father slowly stood and walked towards the front. The pastor walked back and sat down as Joaquín's father stood to face the people. He stood there without saying a word for a few minutes. Everyone sat still as tears ran down his face.

"I want to thank everyone for showing up. My son was loved by a lot of people. I don't like to talk in front of people but I wanted to read something."

Then Joaquín's father reached into his pocket and pulled out a folded paper. He slowly opened it and said, "This is a poem that my son wrote a few days before he died. I want to share it with all of you."

"Qué vive la Raza, y qué vive Zapata.
Simón, it's puro Brown Pride.
I'm ready to die for my gente
but sometimes in the midst of my confusion
I forget what I stand for.
Like when they shanked my camarada in cold blood
for being on the wrong side of town.
And in the midst of confusion

DAVID ROCHA

I loaded up my cuete
with tears falling
I wanted to kill all them vatos from the other Barrio
Not because he was Brown
but because he shot my camarada.
I'm sure you can understand.
At least that's how I saw it,
in the midst of my confusion.
I would yell out,
"What barrio are you from!"
¡Nosotros Controlamos Todo!
And in the midst of my confusion,
of not having money to take care of the ones I loved
selling yerba and crank felt like the best thing I could do.
Simón, it felt good to buy my jaina things other people had.
It felt firme to know that I would be able to take care
of my Jefitos.
But in the midst of my confusions
I didn't let myself see what I was doing to my own Raza.
And in the midst of my confusion,
when I had nowhere to live,
I didn't hesitate to hit up a vato,
pull out my cuete, and demand the feria.
I'm not proud of doing these things,
I didn't even like the feeling of it.
My jefitos brought me up with respect, but
sometimes it feels like it's the only way for survival
for me and for many other vatos.
And in the midst of confusion
it's easy to forget what's right or wrong.
Or just simply after a certain point
it just doesn't matter what's right or wrong.

So I'd rather die than to see my loved one's hungry, ese.
But sometimes in the midst of my confusion
I forget
Que la Raza vive
Que Zapata vive
and that I'm down for Brown Pride.
La vida loca is a hard road, vato
but I'll keep walking
searching
for the end.
Or maybe God forbid
there is no end."

Joaquín's father stopped reading. Then he looked at Joaquín's casket and looked up toward the heavens. "I love you son, and I am proud of you."

Contacts
HOUSE of REST Church
1231 8th Street, Suite 300 Modesto CA 95354
www.houseofrestchurch.com
Email: houseofrestchurch@gmail.com

Book Summary

I want to thank you for listening to this book. Even though it was written years ago, I was really excited about releasing it as an eBook, Audiobook and once again a paperback. I don't know your life, those of you out there reading this. If you lived a life similar to this book, then you know that it is real. For those of you reading this, that don't know this type of life. Even though this book is fiction, these things do happen all of the time. It didn't have to end the way it did. My own life was a rough life, very similar in many aspects to Joaquin. I just want to share with you, that if this is you. If you are lost in the Midst of your Confusion, there is an answer. That answer is Jesus Christ. I said at the beginning of this book that this is what happened to me. This can also happen to you. All you have to do is surrender. I don't agree with the statement of 'I accepted Jesus Christ as my Lord and Savior.' I think a more fitting way is to surrender your life to Jesus Christ. He's the only one that can take the heart of stone out and give you a heart of flesh. He says in Scripture that old things will pass away, and all things will become new. You are a new creation in Christ. You can do it right now... wherever you are at in this world. In your own words, in your own way.

To say, "Lord, I surrender. I surrender my life to you from this day forward. I repent of everything I've done in the past and I want to do things for you from now on. I believe that you died on the cross and after three days, I believe that you rose again. I ask you, as a risen God, as a risen savior to live in my heart, and change me. From this day forward, I will serve you all the days of my life."

And if you pray a prayer like that. Meaning it with all of your heart. Things will change. Weight will come off of you and chains will be broken. I promise this to you. If you did surrender, I want to know about it. All you have to do is email me at houseofrestchurch@gmail.com. Share your story with me. God bless you. Thank you. We have more books coming. I pray that you continue to listen in the future. Thank you

David Rocha

God's fingerprints Cover

God's Fingerprints – A Story of a Pastor's Son
Written by Alfonso Gomez & David Rocha
Available on all book formats: Paperback, eBook &
Audible

God's Fingerprints Book Excerpt

My name is Alfonso Gomez, and this is my story. In writing this, I didn't quite know where to begin, because I quickly realized that I needed to, in a sense, set the stage. So many things were happening around the world, and especially in the United States during this time. Allow me to set the foundation for what life was like in the early 1980s for a young Latino growing up in northern California. Ronald Reagan was elected President of the United States in 1981, and this brought one of the most aggressive policies on the 'war on drugs.' It was sweeping across the nation. Thus, creating a culture within a culture known as the cholo lifestyle. Mexican Americans that had a certain way to dress, a certain slang, and pride that rivaled those in military ranks. It was like a giant black cloud that I had no idea was about to hover over the fields and small towns of the central valley. Prison gang wars were erupting behind the walls and the politics of it was about to explode in the streets, leaving pools of blood and bullet casings across many neighborhoods in the central valley of California.

In looking back, I believe that I was born into a very broken family. It was 1982 and we lived in the projects of west side Modesto. I am not sure how it happened, but one day a woman shared the gospel of Jesus Christ with my mom. This was a big problem, culturally speaking because my dad and mom came from a long line of Catholics that dated back generations. Yet, even amid this, my mom accepted Jesus Christ into her heart and became a Christian. Knowing that my dad would have never allowed it. My mom followed Christ in secret and could never fellowship or go to a Christian church. Yet, even though she herself could never go to a church, she would send my older half-brother to the church by lying to my dad. She would tell him that he was going to visit his aunt that lived in Modesto, yet the entire time he was in a Christian church service each Sunday. She was afraid that my dad would have rejected her, or maybe even kill her. Not much time passed that her confession to follow Christ and be a Christian would be out in the open. Her entire family turned their back on her. I realize now the huge price she paid to follow her heart in serving Christ outside of the Catholic church.

Two years had passed with my mom as a Christian and my dad wanting nothing to do with her Christianity, her church, her pastors or her 'hallelujahs'. They had moved out of Modesto and went a few miles south on Highway 99 to the small town of Turlock. We lived in a small apartment in a predominately Chicano and Mexican neighborhood. I have early memories of my dad and uncles drinking alcohol and hanging out. I am not saying the apartment was a mess, but when I think back, I remember beer cans and trash. One of my uncles was cartel *mafioso* related and was very tough and violent. Eventually, he was sent to federal prison for eight years for drug trafficking. Then deported back to Mexico after serving his sentence in federal prison.

July 7, 1984, is a day my mom will never forget. The marriage was falling apart. I believe my mom felt that the end was coming near for the family. What she didn't know was that my dad was planning to walk out on her and the entire family for good that day. He was literally getting ready in the bathroom to leave with my uncle and go to Tijuana Mexico. I believe it was out of desperation for her family, so she decided to invite the pastors over to speak to my dad. She was afraid and had no idea how he would react. Was he going to flip out? Was he going to walk out on them? I believe she was brave and found a strength within herself because it was God's appointed time. When the pastors knocked on the door and she let them in, it was as if all time stood still. One of the pastors, named Jose, played a major role in my story years later. I wholeheartedly believe that the talk was more than just bible verses because my dad wouldn't have sat down to hear a sermon. Even though I wasn't in the room. I believe that the words from the pastor's mouth were orchestrated by the Lord Himself because my dad sat down with them and allowed the pastor to speak. So, when my dad sat there with these men, something began to tug at his heart. The pastor asked my dad if he could pray for him, and my dad said "Yes." I don't know what words he said in his prayer, but it shook everything within my dad. From the stories I have heard about my dad, it was amazing that he even allowed them to pray for him. And it was there, in my small kitchen, that my dad accepted and surrendered his life to Jesus Christ.

Lost in the Storm cover

Lost in the Storm – From Prison to the Pulpit
By David Rocha
Coming 2019

Lost in the Storm book excerpt

Lock it down now!" echoed loudly through the pod. I tried my hardest to ignore the yelling. "I said lock it down!" demanded the officer.

Unable to continue reading, I put down my Bible and sat up from my bunk. I slowly walked over to my cell door to look out my thin window and into the pod. An argument was quickly escalating as Rico refused to lock down after his hour of pod time. *I know what comes next, I* dreaded.

"My hour isn't up! I was on the phone with my grandmother! And you can't even warn me! You just shut the phones off!" screamed Rico at the top of his lungs.

Rico pulled his shirt off, ready to do battle. The officer stood on the opposite side of the thick glass, looking into the half-circle pod with eighteen cells. Within minutes I knew officers would come rushing in with riot gear: billy clubs and flash bang grenades. Rico began pacing the pod like an angry lion, psyching himself up for the inevitable. *What does it matter anyway since he's facing twenty to life for murder? I* thought. I whispered a prayer for him.

Life in solitary confinement is inhuman. The

hatred it breeds boils like lava ready to explode at the smallest disrespect. Nerves are always on edge and fuses are short. I was about to witness another eruption.

"Here they come! Here they come!" yelled someone from a cell in the top tier. Ten officers dressed in black riot gear complete with shields and masks stood ready at the door to rush in. By this time Rico had run into his cell, came out with bottles of shampoo from the commissary, and began pouring it on the floor next to each door, making it slippery for the officers as they rushed in. The first officer was holding a rifle with flashbangs.

"Come on! I'll take one of you down!" yelled Rico as he balled his fists, ready to swing.

The door popped open and the officer shot the flashbang toward Rico. Instantly the pod was filled with smoke, giving it the effect of a war zone. The officers rushed in screaming "Lay down!" Every inmate began pounding their doors and yelling, which made the entire moment seem like a madhouse. Rico swung and connected with the head of the first officer, sending his face shield flying across the pod. The second officer swung and hit Rico with his baton. Adrenaline and rage were so high that the blow didn't even faze him. Rico's muscles ripped with veins pulsing as if hot venom was traveling throughout his body. Rico somehow grabbed an officer in a chokehold and tried his hardest to squeeze the life out of him. With gritted teeth, he hollered, "All I wanted was to say goodbye! See what you made me do!"

"Let him go! Let him go now!" one officer screamed. The pounding from the inmates became louder. Officers began hitting his legs, back, and arms with their batons. The blows only enraged him more, causing his squeeze on the officer's neck to get tighter. The officer began to turn purple and his eyes began rolling into his head. With no other alternative, an officer pulled back his baton and hit Rico square on the back of his head. The sound of the baton to skull seemed to override all other sounds. Rico's hold released as he fell forward, unconscious. The officers swung and struck a few more blows at his limp body, then cuffed him and carried him off.

As quickly as it began, it ended. The only evidence was a smoke-filled pod. The inmates stopped yelling and kicking their doors, and all was eerily silent. With more frustration than shock, I sat back down on my bunk. "When will this nightmare end?" I asked myself. I was thankful there was an end for me. Some men I've met will never walk into freedom. I at least had a release date. It's unbelievable how many times in the past this could have been a permanent home for me, but God had other plans even though I didn't know it. Let me rephrase that: I knew God had plans for me; I just chose to ignore Him.

We find God in places we'd least expect. Moses found God in the backside of the desert, watching his father-in-law's sheep. Peter found God while pulling up to shore with empty nets after a long night of hard work. A criminal found God while he was being crucified next to Him on a hill named Golgotha. Isaiah 55:8 says, "for my thoughts are not your thoughts, neither are your ways my ways." The same rings true today. We find God on battlefields thousands of miles from home, on deathbeds, in car accidents, through lost jobs, or after the death of a loved one. God seems to show up during our darkest and most hopeless times, as a light showing us the path. In actuality, God has always been there; we just weren't looking.

That brings us to my story. I didn't find God in a church or a parking lot revival. I found Him in solitary confinement, a place more commonly known as "the hole." The phrase "found God" isn't actually correct, however, because to find God implies that God was lost; it's us sinners who are the lost sheep. So the correct term should be "He found me." After years of running and hiding from Him, I slammed right into Him in prison.

It was evening in this hell on earth, tucked inside the massive compound. The jail was surrounded by fences and razor-sharp barbed wire. I was beyond several steel doors and the general population pods, deep inside the building through the long, silent corridors. The "hole" was filled with murderers, rapists, mafia gang leaders, cop killers, drug cartel members and your average violent anti-social maniac who can't be housed in general-population pods because they were too vicious, too manipulative, or too powerful.

I and others alongside me were housed in single cells, which means we had no cellmates. We were kept from one another like Siamese Fighting Fish. We each got one hour outside our cells twice a week, but still within the locked pod. It was the only time we could shower, shave, and use the payphone. We each took turns coming out on an hourly rotation. Two inmates were never out together because allowing contact could have been fatal. Rapists, child molesters, rival gangs and rival drug dealers, as well as racists, were automatically targeted.

We were fed three times a day through slots in the centers of our cell doors. My cell was built with a toilet and sink combination, a concrete table, a metal stool welded to the floor, and a concrete bed with a mattress thinner than my Bible. I had a limited view of the outside through a narrow piece of five-inch glass. I seldom looked outside since my view was composed of a fence, barbed wire, and sky.

Through a control booth, officers monitored six different pods built into a circle around them. This monitoring system wasn't always successful, however, with so many pods and inmates to watch. Men found ways to hang themselves and not be discovered for hours. One of my friends did it before I was put in "the hole." I still pray for his family and try not to think of the times we laughed and talked of the day we'd be free. That was before he was sentenced to life. That night he called his family and said goodbye, walked to his cell, and hanged himself. He was found dead the next morning.

I am in no way encouraging suicide, but I can see how dark and twisted a mind can become in a place like "the hole," where hope means nothing and the sane can quickly go insane. It is the belly of the beast, the gates of hell itself. Without God, we have no chance against Satan. This is Satan's playground: his games, his rules, and he plays for keeps.

Spending days, weeks, and months sitting in a cell alone does something to the human mind. I've seen strong-willed men mentally break. They begin talking to themselves, barking like dogs or screaming for hours as they sit in a dark cold cell week after week. I've learned how to spot a man on the verge of losing reality. He first begins to talk differently and walk differently; I can almost sense him withdrawing into himself. Others fight going insane with anger and hatred. They'll lose all remorse and compassion because it's easier not to care. So they learn to have no mercy.

Officers approached us with caution and fear. We were shackled to our visits, shackled to the nurse, and shackled to court. We were treated as animals, so most of us began to act like animals. I was in constant spiritual battle daily.

Even in Christ I felt suffocated by the evil presence in the "hole." I constantly prayed for strength. I longed to fellowship with another Christian for support. I longed to hold my children, who I haven't touched in two years; I fought to stay afloat in the lake of despair. Sometimes I would realize days had passed since I'd last spoken to anyone. Sleeping became a challenge between the yelling, cursing, arguing, screaming, door banging, and meals. Sometimes even getting a full night's sleep became impossible.

In the beginning of my incarceration, I cherished my sleep; it was the only way to escape my surroundings and situation. I'd dream of my family and the fun times we'd had. Later my dreams turned into nightmares of corpses, death, disasters, violence, pain, and terror. I woke up shaking in fear because I had nightmares of demons chasing me through a forest with no end. *What is happening to me?* I thought. So I started praying for Jesus to watch over me while I slept. I didn't know what was worse, being awake in the living horror of "the hole" or living through the horrors in my mind while I slept. It's impossible to fully describe how it feels to be isolated from the world.

The Kingdom of God book cover

The Kingdom of God
By David Rocha
Coming 2019

The Kingdom of God book excerpt

As I begin to write this book, I realize why I feel so prompted to publish it quickly. Simply put, I wish this book was written for me when I first surrendered my life to Jesus Christ on February 25th, 2004 in a prison cell in solitary confinement. I have been living a life for Christ for the past thirteen years and still didn't have a clear definition or understanding of the Kingdom of God. And not only serving Christ but a graduate from Bible College CLU (Christian Leadership University) with a degree in Biblical Studies and ministry. Also, to add to my thirteen years in Christ, and a degree in Biblical Studies, I have pastored a church that began in the basement of my home in 2011, and slowly have moved from there to various buildings and we are now currently in the very center of the city of Modesto CA operating as the House of Rest Church.

I did not have the typical upbringing of a pastor due to my incarceration. I spent my first six years in Christ behind the wall of federal prison. During that time, I felt as if I was not going to have the proper training to be a pastor, yet I felt called by God to be a pastor and teacher. Most pastors were trained under the wing of elders and pastors, groomed for years before they themselves are launched out to start a new work. Yet, I had no type of leadership, pastor, elder to learn from, which I thought was a bad thing, yet once I released in January of 2010, I realized very quickly that God had called me and many more for such a time as this. Allow me to explain. I came out of prison with a different perspective of what a Christian life should look like. In prison, we shared our lives with the brethren, we shared our food, our books, our dreams, and fears. We would gather together at the same table for breakfast, go to our jobs, meet again for lunch, go back to work then at the end of the day we would have dinner and then meet for Bible study. This was every day. We shared verses we had read and asked each other for opinions. When there was tragedy back home for one of the brothers, we would gather around him in love and pray for him, become a shoulder for him to cry on. When there was something good that happened to a brother or if a brother was about to be released, we would have a party for him in the chapel and use whatever we could get from the commissary to give him a great farewell. We would cry together as we would pray one last time together before one of us would transfer or go home. A fellow brother in Christ would never go hungry, because whatever I had in my locker was theirs, and what was theirs, was mine. Once a month we would each get paid for the job we had and it would go into our inmate account. And on that commissary day, which was each Thursday, each of us would give a tithe (10%) of our income to buy hygiene for anyone that came into the prison. It was a way for us 'the church' to reach out to all that came in, no matter what race or belief they were. They would receive a toothbrush, toothpaste, shower shoes, shampoo, soap, deodorant, and other necessities.

We were a 'church', we had no doubt about that. But we

had no church name, no billboards, no glossy flyers, no website, no social network page and no competing church building down the street. We had no mission statement or vision statement except the great commission. We had no business plan on how to expand the church attendance or gimmicks on how to get people into our group. We simply shared our lives with each other and tried our hardest to be a living example to the rest of the inmates that Jesus can change the heart of a man. The best part in sharing the gospel to everyone was the fact that none of the brothers could ever exalt himself above anyone else, because we were all inmates, all sentenced by a judge and all serving time for something we did wrong. To wake up in a cell or a dorm was a daily reminder of our past. We could not hide from it.

When I released from the BOP (Bureau of Prisons) I did not realize I was going to have a rude awakening of 'Christianity'. I saw a competitive spirit in churches, even within a church many were scrambling within ministries to one-up the next man or woman. I saw pastors act more like a king with his congregation being his subjects under him. Each church or ministry was a kingdom unto itself. I saw many lift their church name or ministry as if it was more important than lifting the name of Jesus. I saw many that were financially blessed in the same building with others that were clearly in need. It was the most disheartening thing I had ever seen. I didn't realize how things were in the outside world, and I wondered how I would fit in this type of self-exalting, build your own kingdom type of Christian life. A verse quickly came to my heart that always resonated with me the entire time I was incarcerated.

Isaiah 42:8 (NKJV)

8 I am the Lord, that is My name;

And My glory I will not give to another,
Nor My praise to carved images.

In this verse, the Lord is speaking to the prophet Isaiah, and very clearly tells us that the Glory of God is His and His alone. We are not to glorify ourselves, our works, our churches, our ministries or our own kingdoms. The Glory is His and His alone.

Always With You book cover

Always With You – a novel inspired by the feature film
Coming Soon
The Feature film is free to view on Youtube
Always With You – Official Film HD